"Y

gave Butler

gambler pulled the trigger as Dutch was bringing his gun around. The bullet punched the man in the chest, dead center.

The other, Ben, saw his partner stagger back and land on the bed, blood blossoming on his chest. He tried to bring his gun around but he was too slow. The gambler drilled him through the heart, and Ben fell dead on the floor, virtually at his partner's feet.

Butler heard footsteps in the hall and turned in time to see Three-Eyed Jack appear in the doorway, gun in hand. Jack surveyed the scene and lowered his gun.

"Looks like I got here too late to help," he said, holstering his weapon.

"I appreciate the gesture."

"Know who these Jaspers are?"

"Not a clue."

"This happen to you before?"

"Once or twice."

"Always strangers?"

"Usually."

Jack shook his head. "Why do I get the feeling you got hell on your trail?"

Books by Robert J. Randisi

THE GAMBLERS

Butler's Wager

THE SONS OF DANIEL SHAYE

Pearl River Junction
Vengeance Creek
Leaving Epitaph

ROBERT J. RANDISI

THE GAMBLERS
BUTLER'S WAGER

HARPER

An Imprint of HarperCollinsPublishers

This is a work of fiction. Names, characters, places, and incidents are products of the author's imagination or are used fictitiously and are not to be construed as real. Any resemblance to actual events, locales, organizations, or persons, living or dead, is entirely coincidental.

HARPER

An Imprint of HarperCollins*Publishers*
10 East 53rd Street
New York, New York 10022-5299

Copyright © 2007 by Robert J. Randisi
ISBN: 978-0-06-089017-9
ISBN-10: 0-06-089017-7

First Harper paperback printing: April 2007

Visit Harper paperbacks on the World Wide Web at
www.harpercollins.com

10 9 8 7 6 5 4 3 2 1

THE GAMBLERS
BUTLER'S WAGER

CHAPTER 1

———◦◉◦———

Tyrone Butler stared at the three aces in his hand and kept his face completely blank. He'd learned a hard lesson years ago not to let your hand show on your face. He'd spent a lot of years playing losing poker before he got the hang of it. Now he was confident that there was no one in the world who could read him.

"How many, Mr. Butler?" the dealer asked.

Butler plucked the mismatched cards from his hand and dropped them facedown on the table.

"Two."

The dealer slid two cards across the table, then turned his attention to the next player. Now down to four players, the crowd of people around the table leaned in. The game had attracted more attention as the night went on, and as the stakes got higher. There had been many poker games in the Gold Room over the years but, of late, Wichita—like Ellsworth, Abilene, Dodge City, and others—had fallen on hard times. Once they had been booming destinations for cattlemen and gamblers, but now the action had moved further west. Even several years ago, at the end of the 1870s, newspapers like the *Wichita Eagle* and the *Dodge City Times* were sounding the death knell for these towns. These days they were inhabited more by farmers than anything else. That was why the men in the saloon were happy to have something to watch, even though only one of the four men was a well-known gambler.

That famous gambler was not Tyrone Butler, but a man called Three-Eyed Jack. He didn't have three eyes, naturally, and nobody knew how'd he'd come to have that name, but at the moment he was the best-known gaming man in town. Of course, he paled in comparison to the Ben Thompsons or Luke Shorts of the world. That was why Three-Eyed Jack preferred to remain a big fish in a small pond.

But tonight Jack wasn't faring well. Two other men had long since busted out of the game, and the stranger to Wichita, Ty Butler, was cleaning house.

There were still two other players at the table, both locals. One was Peter Sutter, who owned Sutter's General Store, and the second, the dealer at the moment, was Sam Troy, a young man who fancied himself a Gambler, with a capital "G." His father owned one of the banks in town, and financed his son's gambling habit. Because the young man never worried about losing money, he had never learned any of the nuances of the game. He simply bet big and tried to buy every pot.

That strategy was not working this evening, because Butler and Three-Eyed Jack were real gamblers, and were not put off by big money bets.

Sutter came next and drew one card. Butler figured him for trying to fill a straight or a flush. He'd been chasing all night and only dumb luck had kept him in the game this long.

Three-Eyed Jack drew three cards, so no secret there. He was trying to improve on a pair.

Finally, Sam Troy dealt himself two cards. He had a habit of keeping a high kicker and then betting big. Butler hoped he drew a hand this time, because he was ready to take the young man.

"You opened, Butler," Troy said. "Whataya do?"

Butler hesitated, hoping to give the impression that he was not sure what he wanted to do.

"I'll go a hundred." It was not a big bet but he could see by the smirk on Troy's face that he had him, so it was enough.

"I think I'm done," Pete Sutter said. He tossed in his cards and rubbed his face so hard it seemed as if he was trying to smooth away the lines he'd earned over his sixty years on this earth.

"I'll raise a hundred," Three-Eyed Jack said.

Butler looked at him. Not a big bet, either. He had the feeling he and Jack were both laying for Troy.

"Well, boys," Troy said, "it looks to me like the price of poker has gone up. I'm gonna raise five hundred."

"You raisin' to five hundred," Jack asked, "or actually raisin' five hundred?"

Momentarily confused—and apparently in possession of none of his father's banking acumen—Troy stared at Jack, then said, "I'm puttin' in his hundred, your hundred, and another five hundred."

"Ah," Butler said, "he's raising five hundred."

"Ain't that what I said?"

Butler and Jack exchanged a glance, and Ty knew he and Three-Eyed were working the kid together.

"All right," he said, "I'll see your five hundred and raise you five hundred."

"After you only bet a hundred?" Troy asked.

"I was testing the waters," Butler said. "What do you say, Jack?"

"I say his five, your five," Jack replied, "and five more."

A gasp went up from the crowd of onlookers.

"Glad I'm out of this hand," Pete Sutter said.

"You guys are both bluffin'," Troy said.

"Five hundred's a big bluff bet, kid," Jack said. "If I was you, I'd believe one of us."

"Well," Troy said, "you ain't me, are ya?" He gathered up his chips and cash and pushed it into the pot. "I got five thousand there. That's the bet."

Butler looked down at his chips and cash. He could easily cover that bet, but when he or Jack won the hand—as he knew one of them would—Sam Troy was going to be one very pissed-off banker's son.

"That all you got?" Butler asked.

"That's it, that's my poke," Troy said, jutting his chin out pugnaciously.

"Well then ... I'll just call."

He pushed in a combination of chips and paper money, then looked at Three-Eyed Jack.

"Jack?"

"Well," Jack said, stroking his long, gray stubbled jaw, "you called him, so I'll get to see his cards, but it's really you I'm worried about, not him."

"You better be worried about me," Troy said.

"No, son," Jack said, "we both got you beat."

"Like hell you do!"

Jack looked at Butler, who just shrugged.

"You wanna bet?" Jack asked.

"I already bet."

"I mean do you want to make a side bet?"

"Side bet ... for what?" Troy asked, confused.

"I say we both have you beat," Jack said. "Do you wanna bet?"

"I got no more money on me."

"I'll take your marker," Jack said. "Your father'll stand good for it, won't he?"

"He damn well will!" Troy said. "How much?"

"Take it easy on yourself," Jack said. "We'll keep it to another five thousand."

"You old bastard, you're tryin' ta buy this hand."

"If you think that, take the bet."

"I'll not only take it, I'll double it. Ten thousand says I got you and him beat."

"Ten?"

"What's the matter," Troy asked. "Too big a bet for you?"

"I'm just not sure your father will cover that much—"

"He'll cover it! Ask anybody."

The men in the circle around the table began to nod.

"All right, then," Jack said. "I'll take that bet." He looked at Butler. "What about you?"

"He'd never cover me, too," Butler said.

"Like hell!" Troy said. "I'll cover you, too."

"Ten grand?" Butler asked.

"That's right."

"Who's got paper and pencil?" Butler asked.

The bartender came forward and gave Troy a pencil and some paper. He wrote each man a marker for ten thousand dollars. These were put on the side, as they were not part of the main pot.

"It was your raise, kid," Butler said to Troy. "What've you got?"

Sweating, Troy put his cards down on the table. Three queens. The other two cards were lower. No kicker this time. He'd held his three queens.

"No good," Butler said. He placed his hand on the table. He'd drawn a pair of deuces to go with his three Aces. A full house. A murmur went up from the crowd.

"You only won the pot," Troy reminded him. "The markers say you both gotta beat me."

"That's what they say, all right," Jack said, and set his cards down. Amazing. He'd kept a pair of kings and had drawn a third. He had three kings.

"You're beat, boy," he said. "Pot and side bets. The pot's yours, Mr. Butler, and here's your marker."

Jack tossed Butler's marker into the pot and the man raked it all in.

"Wait a minute, wait a minute!" Troy said. "You both set me up."

"What?" Jack asked.

"How come every time I made a big bet tonight one of you called me?" he demanded.

"Because you made big bets all night with nothing, kid," Butler said. "You can't buy every pot."

"It's not all about the money, son," Jack said. "If you bet a lot, you better have the hand to back it up."

Troy stuck his lower lip out like a small boy.

"That usually works."

"Against tinhorns and farmers, maybe," Jack said.

"Not against poker players," Butler added.

Troy glared at both men, then stood up so quickly he knocked over his chair. He was wearing a new-looking Colt in an equally new-looking leather holster. Butler thought he'd been smelling new leather all night. Now he knew why.

Troy's hand hovered near his gun.

"I wanna know why you two are always callin' my big bets!" he demanded. "Yer workin' together."

"Calm down," Jack told him. "I never met this gent before tonight."

"Take it easy, kid," Butler said.

Troy *was* a kid, in his twenties, probably five or six years younger than Butler, and ten or fifteen younger than Three-Eyed Jack. If he was going to live past this night, however, he was going to have to become calm and not draw his gun.

Troy got up and cleared away, backing into the crowd, then the crowd as a whole moved further back.

"I don't lose like this," Troy said.

"Son," Jack said, "I'll bet you'd lose all the time if you played with poker players, and not farmers."

If this was an insult to the crowd, they didn't react.

"Now, don't pull that hogleg," Jack said. "I don't know about Mr. Butler, here, but I'm pretty fast with a gun. Mr. Butler?"

"I can hold my own," Butler said.

"See?" Jack said. "One of us would surely kill you if you pull that weapon."

"I'll take one of you fuckers with me!" Troy snarled.

"You don't want to die, kid," Butler said. "Think about it."

"It ain't worth it," Jack said, then he went too far. "Tell you what. If you settle down, Mr. Butler or me can give you some lessons."

"I don't need any goddamn lessons!" Troy shouted.

Butler moved then, because Troy looked directly at Jack. He grabbed the near edge of the table and shoved. The other edge caught Troy in the hips, and Butler kept pushing, digging his toes in. Troy stepped backward to try to retain his balance, and that's when Jack moved. He leaped to his feet, reached out, and snatched the young man's gun from his holster.

"Hey!" Troy shouted, righting himself.

Butler gave way to anger.

"You stupid little sonofabitch!" he snapped. "One of us could've gotten killed just because you're a god-damned sore loser."

"You can't—" Troy started, but Butler came around the table and threw a punch. The blow struck Troy on the nose, which squashed like a tomato, blood spurting everywhere. Troy staggered back and fell onto the floor in a seated position, both hands smacked over his face.

"You bwoke my dose!" Troy cried.

"It's a lot less than you deserve," Jack said, tucking Troy's gun into his own gun belt. "Now, get the hell out of here."

Troy staggered to his feet, looked at Jack and said, "I wan' my gun."

"I'll leave it with the sheriff," Jack said. "Have your father collect it from him in the mornin'."

Troy stared at Jack, glared at Butler, then picked up his hat and went out through the batwing doors.

"Game over?" Jack asked Butler.

"I think so."

"Come on, then," the other man said. "I'll buy you a drink."

CHAPTER 2

———◆———

The crowd dispersed, some leaving, some finding their way to tables or the bar. Three-Eyed Jack and Butler claimed two places at the bar and each ordered a beer.

"That was close," Jack said, lifting his mug. "I thought one of us was gonna have to kill him."

"It would have been a shame," Butler said, hefting his own beer. "He's young, and he has time to learn."

"Well, if he don't learn soon," Jack said, "he's not gonna live much longer. A Ben Thompson or Luke Short might not have our patience."

"Let's hope he doesn't find his way into a game with them."

"Where's tomorrow gonna find you, Butler?" Jack asked. "You ain't gonna stay around here."

"Why not?"

"Well," Jack said, "for one thing there ain't room for both of us. And for another, you're too young and this town is dyin'. I figure you to move on to someplace with more life in it."

"I was giving Tombstone some thought," Butler said,

"but from what I hear the Earps have moved in there and are having some problems."

"Well," Jack said, "it would certainly have more life than this place."

"I'm going to hit Dodge City first," Butler said, "on my way west."

"Another dyin' town," Jack said, "but it has more life than this place. I understand Jim Masterson is a lawman there."

"Maybe I'll get to meet Bat, then."

"The way I hear it, Jim and Bat ain't exactly on speakin' terms," Jack said. "Besides, Bat's already in Tombstone with the Earps."

"Well then, maybe I will head there," Butler said, "but right now I think I'll head to bed."

"So early?"

"Gonna get an early start in the morning," Butler said. He drained his beer and set the empty mug down on the bar. "Thanks for the beer."

"Thanks for the game," Jack said. "You made it more interestin' than usual. Less profitable, but more interestin'."

"Why don't you leave Wichita, Jack?" Butler asked.

"Naw, not me," Jack said. "I'm close to fifty now. Time for me to stay in one place."

Butler was surprised. Three-Eyed Jack did not look fifty to him.

"Fifty ain't so old."

"My bones feel older," Jack said. "They won't let me get on a horse for any period of time. Nah, Wichita's good enough for me, right now."

"Well, I'll leave you to it, then," Butler said.

"Good luck headin' west," Jack said. "You got some big games ahead of you. I can see it."

"Thanks, Jack," Butler said, "and good night."

Butler hit the dark, quiet street and headed for his hotel. He left the lights and sounds of the Main Street saloons behind him. When the shot rang out it was as if he'd anticipated it. He was already rolling in the street when the bullet struck the dirt where he'd been standing. Fact was, Butler was always expecting a shot, and his reflexes had saved his life more than once.

He came to a stop on one knee, Colt in hand. He was waiting for a second shot so the muzzle flash would give him a target, but it didn't come. Nobody came out to see what was happening, either. One shot on the streets of Wichita did not rate investigation. He remained stock-still, watching the doorways and alleys for movement, or shadows.

His hotel was two blocks away. In his experience a man willing to fire one shot is more than willing to fire a few more. He didn't think he was going to make the two blocks without another try.

He knew the shooter was not young Sam Troy. For one thing Jack had his gun, and though Troy could have gotten himself another one, Butler was pretty sure they'd convinced him of the error of his ways, at least for tonight.

He didn't holster his gun. If the shooter was who he thought it was, he was going to need it. Not that he knew the exact identity of the shooter. It would be just another in a long line of men trying to collect on a bounty. This was no law-appointed bounty, but one that had followed him from back East. It had been years since his family had been killed in Philadelphia, and as the only one left, Ty Butler still had a price on his head, put there by ... somebody.

His father, a wealthy investor from Philadelphia, had sent him west to keep him safe. He had only been gone a month or so when word reached him that his father, uncles, and other family members had all been murdered. Luckily, his mother had died of natural causes years before, and so escaped the slaughter.

Eager to return home to seek vengeance, his father's lawyer and long-time friend had convinced him to remain in the West.

"You'll be dead before you get both feet off the train," the man told him in a letter. "Just keep heading west. They will come after you, and one day you'll take one of them alive. Don't come back here, Ty, unless you are armed with information."

So whoever it was out there in the dark, gunning for him, his goal was to take him alive and squeeze the information out of him about who had hired him. But that didn't mean he wasn't ready to defend himself. He'd already dispatched nine such assassins over the years, not one had allowed themselves to be taken alive.

Sometimes, when months would go by without an attempt, he'd think that maybe they'd given up. Maybe the price had been taken off his head. But allowing himself to be lulled into a false sense of security would have cost him his life, because, eventually, there was always *another* attempt.

Like tonight.

CHAPTER 3

———◆———

The two men at the bar in the Gold Room watched as Tyler Butler faced off against the young kid, with the older gambler backing his play—or the other way around. Either way, the two men had managed to disarm the kid and send him packing.

"Damn," the first man said.

"What?"

"I wanted to see his move."

"What does it matter?" the second man asked. "We're gonna bushwack him, anyway. I'm just glad the kid didn't kill 'im, because then our bounty woulda went up in smoke."

"Still," the first man said, "after hearin' so much about this guy, I kinda wanted to see his move."

Dutch Miller stared at his partner, Ben Johnson, and said, "I tell you what, Ben. You call him out. This way you'll get to see his move. And if he kills you, I'll gun him."

"Sure, you'd like that," Dutch said. "Get to keep the reward for yerself, that way."

"Okay," Dutch said, "so if yer not gonna face 'im, stop your jabberin'. Let's get outside and get ready."

As they headed for the door Ben asked, "What if the other gambler comes out with 'im?"

"If he gets in the way," Dutch said, "we'll do for him, too. Now let's go."

Butler stepped up onto the boardwalk and melted into the shadows. His hotel was on this side of the street, a couple of blocks up. He wondered if the shooter would run ahead to wait for him, or if there'd be a second one there?

In Cleveland a guy had tried for him from a rooftop with a rifle in broad daylight. His mistake. There was a policeman nearby who got to him even before Butler could.

In Chicago one single man had tried for him, but he'd tried it out in the open and Butler had beaten him to the draw.

In St. Jo, Missouri they'd sent two shooters after him. He'd gotten both of them, but not before a lot of running and ducking and taking a bullet in the left arm.

In Abilene, just a month or so ago, three men had tracked him for miles, but they waited too long. By the time they tried for him he'd met up with his friend Mickey O'Day. Between the two of them they'd dispatched the three gunmen, unable to take any of them alive.

Now he was wondering to himself, what was it this time, one or two?

There was a time in Wichita when, on any given night, you wouldn't hear a shotgun blast in the middle of the street because of the noise coming from all the saloons. Even now the patrons in the Gold Room were too busy to hear a single gunshot—all of them except Three-Eyed Jack. His ears were attuned to all sorts of sounds, and he was able to differentiate them from one another. He could hear the piano, the cooing of the saloon girls to the customers, trying to get them to buy another drink or go upstairs. He could hear money or chips hitting the faro table, and the sound of the ball bouncing around on the roulette wheel, looking for a place to rest.

And he knew a single gunshot when he heard one.

Butler made his way along the street toward his hotel, gun in hand. It didn't sound like he was being followed, but as experienced as he got year after year at handling himself in these situations, the assassins were also becoming more and more adept. Sooner or later he was going to run into one who had developed a little more quickly than him, and he'd meet his match and maker on the same night.

But hopefully, not tonight.

"You missed, didn't you?" Dutch asked Ben.

"Yeah, I did," Ben admitted, "but why'd you tell me not to take a second shot if I did?"

"Because I knew you'd miss."

"What? You sayin' you're a better shot than I am?" Ben demanded.

"With a rifle, yeah," Dutch said, "but you got it all over me with a handgun, Ben."

"Then why'd you make me take a shot with a rifle?"

"Because I wanted you to herd him down here, to his

hotel," Dutch explained. "This is where we're gonna take 'im."

"But now he's warned."

"No," Dutch said, "he'll think that kid poker player took a shot and missed. He'll write it off as a drunk sore loser, and he'll go to his room. He'll be there waitin' for us."

"But if he's waitin'—"

"I didn't really mean he'd be waitin' on us," Dutch said quickly. "He'll just be waitin' there for us to kill."

He could tell from Ben's face that the man was totally confused.

"It don't matter," Dutch said. "You do just like I say and we'll earn our bounty tonight."

"Good," Ben said. "I need me some money—Look, that him? Here he comes."

"Just relax," Dutch said. "We got to give him time to get settled."

The one thing Butler wasn't going to do tonight was get settled.

His guess was someone was in the saloon watching him, saw what happened with the banker's son, decided to take a shot at him thinking he'd figure it was the young sore loser. Butler had gotten real good at guessing the intentions of these assassins, and judging solely by the fact that he was still alive, his instincts had yet to fail him.

He finally made his way to the front door of his hotel without further incident and entered carefully. The desk clerk looked up at him curiously as he approached the desk.

"Has anyone been looking for me, today or tonight?" he asked the young man.

"No, sir, Mr. Butler," the man said. "I ain't seen nobody, all day or all night."

"All right," Butler said. "Thanks."

The clerk looked down at the gun, which Butler had forgotten he was holding in his hand.

"Is there some problem, sir?"

"No," Butler said, holstering the weapon. "No problem. At least, not one with the hotel. I'll be checking out come morning."

"Yes, sir. Good night, sir."

Butler went up to his room, hoping that whoever the assassins were they'd come for him soon. He needed to get some sleep if he was going to get an early start.

CHAPTER 4

Dutch and Ben approached the front desk, and as the clerk looked up they stuck both their guns in his face.

"Room number for the gambler, Butler," Dutch said.

"Sir, I cannot—" the clerk started, but Dutch clubbed him with the barrel of his gun, not letting him finish. Even before he hit the ground Dutch had the register book turned around and open.

"Six," he said to Ben. "Let's go."

They crept up the stairs, which creaked audibly beneath their combined weight. Once they reached the top of the stairs they moved single file down the hall toward room six, guns at the ready. When they reached room six, Butler's, they stepped each to one side of the door, then Dutch signaled Ben to kick it in. They'd done this many times before. The best time to catch somebody off guard was when they were in bed, alone or with someone.

Ben stepped back, kicked the door in, and leaped into the room. Dutch came in behind him. They swept the room with their guns ready, but nobody was there.

"What the—" Dutch said.

"Where is the cocksucker?" Ben demanded.

The door to room seven, across the hall, opened, and Butler stepped out, gun in hand.

"You boys looking for me?"

Dutch turned and gave Butler no choice. The gambler pulled the trigger as Dutch was bringing his gun around. The bullet punched the man in the chest, dead center. Shoot for the largest part of the body, Butler had been taught years ago, especially when you have no time to aim.

Ben saw Dutch stagger back and land on the bed, blood blossoming on his chest. He turned and looked at Butler, who said, "Don't," but to no avail. Ben tried to bring his gun around, but he was too slow. The gambler drilled him through the heart, and Ben fell dead on the floor at the foot of the bed, virtually at his partner's feet.

Butler heard footsteps in the hall and turned in time to see Three-Eyed Jack appear in the doorway, gun in hand. He tensed, but realized the man wasn't there to kill him.

Jack surveyed the scene and lowered his gun.

"Looks like I got here too late to help," he said, holstering his weapon.

"I appreciate the gesture."

Jack stepped into the room, checked the two men, found them good and dead.

"Know who these two jaspers are?"

"Not a clue. What tipped you off?"

"I heard a shot in the street. That you?"

"One of them, I guess," Butler said. "Took a shot and missed."

Three-Eyed Jack turned and looked at the door to room seven, which was wide open.

"Looks like you were ready for 'em."

"After that first shot, I'd of been a fool not to be." Butler ejected the spent shells from his gun, replaced them, and holstered it. "Guess the sheriff should be here soon."

"Maybe, maybe not," Jack said. "That'll depend on whether or not he's awake."

"The clerk?"

"They knocked him out, but he's alive."

"Good. We might as well go across to my room, have a drink and wait to see if the law shows up."

"This ain't your room?"

"No."

"Guess they had it wrong."

"I guess so."

They went across to room seven and left the door open. Butler retrieved a bottle of whiskey from a chest of drawers and two glasses. He poured two fingers into each glass and handed Jack one.

"This happened to you before?" Jack asked.

"Once or twice."

"Always strangers?"

"Usually."

Jack took a sip and said, "Why do I get the feeling you got hell on your trail?"

CHAPTER 5

Sheriff Pat Hadley first listened to Butler's story, then heard what Three-Eyed Jack had to say.

"It was self-defense, Sheriff," Jack finished. "Ain't no doubt about that at all."

"Well," Hadley said, scratching his balding head, "I reckon if you say so, Jack."

"What about my say so, Sheriff?" Butler asked.

"Sorry, Mister," the lawman said, "but I don't know you. I do know Jack, here, though. If he says you're okay, I guess that's good enough for me."

Butler looked at Jack, who shrugged.

"One thing's got me puzzled, though," the sheriff admitted.

"And what's that?" Butler asked.

"If they was after you, why'd they kick in that door?"

"Good question," Butler said. "I guess maybe they got the wrong room number."

"Could be," the sheriff said. "Well, I'll get me some boys to carry them bodies out."

The sheriff left room seven and Butler asked Jack, "Another drink?"

"One more ain't gonna hurt nothin'," Jack said.

Ty Butler closed the door and poured them each two fingers more of whiskey.

"Pretty smart move," Jack said.

"What is?"

"Checkin' into one room but stayin' across the hall," Jack said. "All you gotta do is slip the clerk a few extra dollars."

"That what I did?" Butler asked.

Jack shrugged. "Don't matter, I guess. Whatever you got doggin' your trail, it's your business. I think you forgot about somethin', though."

"What's that?"

"That marker the Troy kid gave each of us for ten thousand," Jack told him.

"I figured that was no good," Butler said.

"No, the kid's father will stand good the debt," Jack said.

"I've got to get going at first light," Butler said.

"You gonna walk away from that marker?"

"Not if you'll give me fifty cents on the dollar."

Jack looked surprised.

"Five thousand for a ten thousand marker?"

"Five thousand profit for you."

"You serious?"

"Yep."

"Ain't got that much on me."

"Meet me at the livery stable in the morning," Butler said. "I'll sell it to you then."

"You got a deal, friend."

Jack tossed off the last of his drink and put the glass down on the top of the chest.

"Guess I'll turn in myself, so's I can get up nice and early."

"I'll see you then."

Jack paused as he opened the door and said, "Hope the rest of your night is quiet."

"So do I."

When Butler came out of the livery leading his saddled horse he found Three-Eyed Jack waiting for him outside.

"Nice roan," Jack said. "He got a name?"

"Not really," Butler said. "I just usually call him Stupid."

Jack looked at the horse's face and eyes, and said with a shrug, "It suits him, I guess."

Jack took an envelope out of his pocket and handed it to Butler.

"Five thousand dollars, as agreed."

Butler accepted the envelope and put it in his inside jacket pocket without counting the money. This plus what he had won last night would be a good stake for Dodge City, and his trip west. He took the marker from Sam Troy and handed it over to Three-Eyed Jack. After that the two men shook hands.

"I gotta ask you somethin'," Jack said.

"Go ahead."

"You got a price on your head?"

"Yeah, I guess so, but not from the law."

"Personal?"

"Yes."

"You know how much?"

"No idea."

"How long?"

Butler shrugged. "Years."

"Jesus," Jack said. "Somebody's got a long memory."

"I'm afraid so."

"Well," Jack said, "you're a young man. Maybe you'll just outlive whoever it is."

"At this rate," Butler said, "I doubt it."

He mounted his horse.

"Anybody else comes this way lookin' for you I'll point them in the wrong direction."

"I appreciate that, Jack."

"You might think about changin' your name," Jack said, "if you ain't already."

"I have thought about it," Butler said. "My name's all I got, Jack."

"I can understand that."

Butler nodded, turned his horse and rode out of Wichita.

CHAPTER 6

Dodge City,
April 6, 1881

Jim Masterson looked up as the door to the office opened and former Mad Dog Kelley came walking in, followed by Neal Brown.

"Is it official?" Jim asked.

"As official as it gets," Kelley said. "I'm out as mayor, and you and Neal have been fired."

Ex-City Marshal Jim Masterson frowned. His brother Bat had had his own problems in Dodge and been exiled, and now the same was likely to happen to him. The new mayor, A. B. Webster, was wasting no time in cleaning house.

He looked at his now ex-City Deputy Marshal Neal Brown and said, "Reckon we best clear out of here, Neal."

"I ain't got much to pack," Brown said.

"What about George and Fred?" Jim asked. George Hinkle was sheriff, and Fred Singer undersheriff.

"Both out," Kelley said.

"Who's replacing them?"

"That I don't know," the ex-mayor said. "You boys up for a drink? I'm buyin'."

"Celebratin', Dog?" Jim asked.

"Why not?" Kelley asked. "Our days in Dodge may be numbered. Might as well take the time to celebrate."

"The Lady Gay?" Neal Brown asked.

"As good a place as any," Jim said.

"Not gonna be a problem with Peacock?" Kelley asked.

A. J. Peacock and Jim Masterson had entered into partnership of the Lady Gay several months earlier, and that partnership was teetering on uneasy ground.

"Fuck Peacock," Jim said. "I'm still half owner of the Gay. I'll meet you boys over there as soon as I clear out my desk."

"I'll find George and Fred," Kelley said. "Invite them to join us."

True to his word Neal Brown left the office carrying only his rifle. He truly did not have much to clear out.

Once his friends were gone Jim Masterson sat down for the last time behind his desk. He'd had a decent run, having worn the marshal's badge since November of '79. He wasn't quite ready to leave Dodge, though. He may not have been the law anymore, but he was still owner of the Lady Gay Saloon and Dance Hall—albeit half owner with Peacock.

He didn't know why Peacock was being so pigheaded about his brother-in-law, Al Updegraff. Peacock had hired him as a bartender as soon as they took possession of the Lady Gay, and the man was a lush, guzzling as much free whiskey as he could while he worked. Jim had wanted to fire the man, but Peacock would have none of it, and now Updegraff was a serious bone of contention between the two. Clearly, the man sided with his brother-in-law, and the rift between them was growing—and growing untenable.

Fuck it, he thought, I really do need a drink.

Tyrone Butler came riding down Front Street as Jim Masterson entered the Lady Gay Saloon. Having never been to Dodge before, Butler was impressed by the town's history as "Queen of the Cow Towns." A student of history, he also knew that the title passed from town to town, belonging at one time to Ellsworth and Wichita as well as Dodge. Dodge, however, counted Wyatt Earp and Bat Masterson as part of her history—as well as buffalo hunting, dead lawmen, and plenty of gamblers. It was not only one of the great cow towns, but one of the great gambling towns, with a collection of saloons and dance halls. The Long Branch and Alhambra were famous, the Lady Gay—which he was riding past—just slightly less so. Butler didn't know it, but at one time, back when Wyatt Earp was hired to bring law to Dodge City, there were nineteen establishments in town that served liquor. That number now was significantly less.

But he was pleased to see that the Long Branch and Lady Gay were still in operation. He wanted to play poker in both of those saloons before he left Dodge.

But he'd only just arrived, and he had to see to first things first—like taking Stupid to the livery, and getting himself a hotel room.

* * *

Jim Masterson joined Neal Brown and Dog Kelly at their table, after getting himself a beer from the bar. Thankfully, Al Updegraff was not on duty yet.

"Well," he said, "looks like the first afternoon in a long while we all have time free."

Dog Kelly rubbed his hands over his face.

"At least you fellas have your places," Neal Brown said. They were sitting in Masterson's place, and Dog Kelley owned the Alhambra. In fact, when James "Dog" Kelley first erected the Alhambra on Front Street, it was one of the first buildings in Dodge—there still wasn't much but Front Street. "I don't know what I'm gonna do."

"You can work for me here," Jim Masterson said.

"Or for me at the Alhambra," Kelley said.

"What would I do?" Neal asked. "Tend bar? Be a swamper? I'm a lawman, damn it."

Jim nodded. Aside from owning the Lady Gay he'd worn a badge most of his life. His brother Ed had died right here in Dodge, shot while wearing a badge, and Bat had worn the star in Dodge and other places for years. Maybe it was time to get out from behind the tin star for good.

"Well, I'm gonna put some more of my time into this place."

"Whataya gonna do first?" Neal Brown asked.

"I'm gonna get rid of Al Updegraff."

"I don't think your partner will be too thrilled about that," Kelley said. "How you gonna work that out?"

"I don't know," Jim said. "Peacock's bein' goddamned stubborn about this."

"Put a bullet in the useless bastard," Neal said, speaking of Updegraff, "that oughtta take care of the situation."

"Kill him?" Kelley asked.

"I didn't say kill 'im," Brown said. "Just ... nick 'im a bit, get him off his feet and out from behind the bar."

"I'm tempted," Jim said, "I truly am."

"Why don't you sell out," Kelley said, "come in with me and Pete at the Alhambra?"

Pete Beatty was Kelley's partner, and they got along a lot better than Jim and Peacock did.

"I wouldn't wanna be the cause of you and Pete fallin' out," Jim said. "Naw, I'll stick it out here."

"What about Bat?" Brown asked.

"What about him?"

"You fellas still not talkin'?"

Jim didn't answer. As well as Neal Brown and Dog Kelley knew the Mastersons, neither of them knew the bone of contention that existed between the brothers, at the moment.

"Where is Bat, these days?" Kelley asked.

"Heard he was in Tombstone, with Wyatt," Jim said.

"Tombstone," Brown said. "There's an idea. Think he needs a deputy?'

"Wyatt's the law there, deputy to Virgil, along with Morgan," Jim said. "Don't know that Bat's even wearin' a badge. Doc Holliday's there, too."

"Holliday?" Brown said, with distaste. "Reckon I'll stay here, then. That sonofabitch is crazy."

"So it's back to here, then," Jim said.

"Maybe the new mayor will give you a job, Neal?" Kelley asked. "He's gonna need experienced men."

"Wonder who the new city marshal's gonna be?" Brown asked.

"Guess we'll all just have to wait to find out," Jim said. "You fellas want another beer? I'm buyin'."

"Only if you'll come over to the Alhambra later and allow me to return the favor," Dog Kelley said.

"Done!" Jim said, and headed for the bar to get three more beers.

CHAPTER 7

Tyrone Butler walked along Front Street, wishing he'd been in Dodge eight or ten years ago. He had gotten himself a room at the Dodge House, and was happy to see the Delmonico Restaurant was still open. He decided to go first to the Alhambra for a beer and a look, and then he'd return to the Delmonico for a steak.

While Dodge was no longer the cow town it once was, it was obvious as soon as he walked through the Alhambra doors that the town still attracted the gamblers. The faro, roulette, and craps tables were in full swing, and off in one corner he could see two poker games going.

He went to the mile-long bar and waited for the bartender to make his way from the other end.

"What'll it be?" the man asked.

"Cold beer."

"Comin' up."

The bartender drew a mug of cold beer and carried it over to Butler.

"Gambler?" he asked.

"Does it show?" Butler asked.

"All over you. What's your game?"

"Poker." Butler sipped the beer, found it ice cold.

"You'll find what you want here."

"I'm going to get a steak first."

"The Delmonico," the bartender said. "Can't beat it."

"That's where I was going to go," Butler said, "soon as I finish this beer."

"Well, don't rush it," the barman said. "It's good beer."

Butler sipped his beer and watched some men at the far end of the bar, who seemed to be celebrating.

"What's going on?" he asked the bartender.

"You got here two days after election day," the man said. "We got us a new mayor, and he's cleanin' house. Fired the city marshal, Jim Masterson, his deputy, as well as the sheriff and undersheriff."

"Jim Masterson?"

"Yep," the bartender said, "Bat's younger brother. Been marshal here for a few years, but today he's out. Some folks are kinda excited about that."

"What about you?"

"Not me," the man said. "I like Jim. I think he was a great marshal for this town."

"Do you think they'll replace him with his brother Bat?" Butler asked.

"Not a chance," the bartender said. "Bat ain't in Dodge, but even if he was mayor, Webster would never hire another Masterson."

"What's Jim going to do?"

"Ah, he owns part of the Lady Gay, so I guess he'll concentrate on that. And the old mayor, Dog Kelley? He half owns this place."

"Interesting," Butler said. He looked around. "I don't suppose Masterson is in here now, is he?"

"Naw," the barman said. "My guess is they're over at the Lady Gay. They'll be over here soon enough, though."

"I'll be back later," Butler said. "Maybe I'll spot them."

"Whatever you wanna do," the bartender said. "Interested in a girl for the evening? Maybe the night?"

Butler looked around, saw three or four saloon girls circulating through the room, all of them beautiful.

"I'll let you know."

"You do that. The name's Hogan, Matt Hogan. Jest ask for me I'll get ya whatever ya want."

"I'll remember." Butler finished his beer, set the empty mug down. "See you later, Matt."

"Usually," Hogan said, "when a man introduces himself, the other fella does the same. Common courtesy, ya know?"

"Sorry," Butler said, "I think I left my manners on the trail between here and Wichita. The name's Butler, Ty Butler."

"Came here from Wichita?" Hogan asked, as they shook hands. "Not much goin' on there, huh?"

"Not much," Butler said. "That's why I came to Dodge."

"Well, you'll find everything you want here, my friend Butler."

"I can see that, Matt. Thanks."

Butler left the Alhambra, intending to go to the Delmonico for that steak. On the way he passed the Lady Gay and he noticed two men peering in one of the front windows. There was nothing really unusual about them. They wore trail clothes and guns in worn holsters. But before they entered the saloon they each removed their guns and checked them, to see that they were loaded. In Butler's experience the only time you did that was when you intended to use the gun.

The two men entered through the batwing doors, and Butler's curiosity got the better of him. He followed them in.

CHAPTER 8

Butler stopped just inside the batwing doors. The Lady
Gay was not as large as the Alhambra, but it was
no less lively on this evening. He looked around and
spotted the two men who had entered ahead of him,
one by one. They had split up, one going to the bar,
and the other over to the roulette table to watch the
wheel. Only he wasn't watching the wheel, he had his
eye on a table where three men were sitting. Butler
knew that there was definitely trouble in the air, but
if he went to the three men and tried to warn them,
would they believe him? He knew what it was to be
stalked by assassins, though. If he did warn them,
maybe these fellows would leave and there'd be no
inkling as to who sent them. Butler also knew the frus-
tration of that.

He decided to go to the bar himself, get a beer and
nurse it while keeping an eye on the two men.

"Beer," he told the bartender.

The man nodded, didn't speak to him, and brought
him one. Butler picked it up in his left hand, turned

his back to the bar, leaned against it and watched the floor.

The Lady Gay also had women working the floor, not wearing dresses as fancy as at the Alhambra, and pretty rather than beautiful, but they appeared to be popular nevertheless. Pale skin and overflowing bosoms did wonders for men's thirst and egos.

But the two men who had come in ahead of him were not looking at any of the women, which was another-tip-off. One of them had gotten himself a beer, the other was still at the roulette wheel, both still had their eyes on the three seated men, who seemed oblivious to the danger.

Butler called the bartender over.

"Those three men over there," he asked. "Who are they?"

"Them's three unhappy men, stranger," the bartender said. "One's our ex-marshal, Jim Masterson, with his ex-deputy Neal Brown, and the third, older fella is our ex-mayor, Dog Kelley. They all lost their jobs in the past two days."

"That's too bad," Butler said. "I guess they're drowning their sorrows, huh?"

"Guess you could say that. Listen, I gotta go. My shift is over, but you have yourself a great time. Al will take care of you."

"Yeah, thanks."

The bartenders changed places. The new one was in his late thirties, and he weaved a bit, as if he'd already sampled some of the beer, or whiskey ... or both. Butler was not going to pay any attention to him until he noticed a quick look pass between him and one of the two men who was at the bar. It looked to him like a signal.

What came next happened very quickly. The man at the bar put his beer down and drew his gun. Likewise, the fellow at the roulette wheel turned and pulled his gun.

Butler was surprised to see Jim Masterson jump to his feet, whirl, draw his gun, and plug the man at the roulette wheel before the fellow could get off a shot. Shouts rose up as the body fell on top of the roulette layout. One of the men seated with Masterson jumped to his feet and drew his gun, watching the crowd. The other—the ex-mayor—simply slid from his chair and hit the floor.

Neither Masterson or his ex-deputy saw the man at the bar, so it fell to Butler to draw his gun and stop him.

"Hold it!" he shouted.

The man turned his head briefly to see who had shouted at him. When he saw Butler with his gun out he frowned, but switched his attention back to Masterson, who was in the act of turning to also see who had yelled. Butler had no recourse but to fire, which he did. The bullet struck the gunman in the side of the head, drilled through and came out the other side. It kept on going and hit another man, a bystander, in the arm, knocking him off his feet.

There was more yelling, but the shooting was apparently over. Both Masterson and his deputy, Brown, turned their guns on Butler, who was still holding his. They both also saw the man on the floor at the base of the bar. Butler made a show of putting his gun up, holstering it, and showing the ex-lawmen his hands.

"Check him out," Masterson said to Brown, indicating the man on the roulette wheel layout. He, in turn, approached the man at the base of the bar.

It was suddenly quiet in the saloon, men and women clearing out, making room, reminding Butler of the recent scene in the saloon in Wichita.

"Know 'im?" Masterson called out to Brown.

"Never saw him before. That one?"

Jim Masterson used his foot to turn the body over so he could see his face. He had to look at the right side of his face because the bullet had taken most of the left side with it.

"Don't know 'im," he said. "Put up your gun, Neal. It's all over. Dog, you can get up."

He turned and looked at Butler, approached him. The men around Butler cleared away, fearing another exchange of bullets.

"You helped me out, friend," Masterson said. "I'm obliged."

"He was taking a bead on your back, Marshal."

"You know who I am?"

"You were pointed out to me," Butler admitted.

"Name's Jim Masterson," he said, putting out his hand, "and it's ex-marshal."

"Butler's my name." The two men shook hands.

"You wanna join us at our table, wait for the law to show up?" Masterson asked. "I own this place. Drinks 'er on the house."

Butler smiled and said, "Don't think I've had a better offer since I came to town."

"And when was that?" Masterson asked.

"Just about an hour ago."

"You don't believe in wastin' any time, do you?" Jim Masterson asked.

CHAPTER 9

One of the saloon girls brought over four fresh beers while the activity around them got back to normal—except for the two dead bodies. They managed to lift the one off the roulette wheel so they could continue playing, though everyone was careful not to step on him. The same went for the second one by the bar. They just worked around them.

"So you have no idea who those men were?" Butler asked.

"No," Masterson said.

"But we got an idea who sent them," Brown said.

"Neal," Jim Masterson said, warningly.

"Why shouldn't he know?" Brown asked. "He stuck his neck out for us, didn't he?"

"Well, first," Masterson said, "I'd like to know how, and why?"

"I just rode into town a little while ago from Wichita," Butler said. "Put my horse up at the livery, got a room at the Dodge House, had a drink at the Alhambra and was on my way to the Delmonico for a steak."

"So what made you stop in here?" Masterson asked.

"Saw those two loitering around outside, peering in the window," Butler said. "Saw them check their loads before they came in. I figured they were after somebody. When I came in I noticed them casing the three of you. I just decided to keep an eye on them."

"I feel like a fool," Brown said. "I didn't see them."

"Don't feel bad," Masterson told him. "I only saw the one by the roulette wheel."

"I wondered about that," Butler said. "You moved pretty fast when he drew."

"I had one eye on him," Masterson said, "but you saved my bacon with the other one. I'm much obliged."

Butler looked at Brown.

"You said you thought you knew who sent them. Somebody after you because you pack stars?"

"We did pack stars," Brown said, "but not no more—and no, that wouldn't be the reason."

"This ain't the place to talk about it," Masterson said.

"Where is the place to talk it over?" Brown asked.

"My place," Kelley said.

"Dog owns the Alhambra," Masterson said.

"Friendly bartender over there," Butler said to Kelley.

"Which one?"

"Matt Logan."

"Yeah, Matt's a good man."

"Why don't we go over there?' Brown asked. "Just in case somebody in here is getting' ideas."

"I hate bein' run out of my own place," Masterson said.

"You ain't bein' run out," Kelley said. "You already agreed to come to my place for a drink."

"You got a point there, Dog," Masterson said, "but we've got to wait for the law to show up."

"I wonder who it'll be when they do show up?" Brown asked.

As if on cue the batwing doors swung inward and a man wearing a marshal's badge entered.

"I'll be a sonofabitch," Brown said, when he saw the man.

"Fred Singer," Kelley said, "that traitor."

"Traitor?" Butler asked.

"He just got fired, like we did," Brown said. "He was undersheriff."

"And now it looks like he's the new city marshal," Jim Masterson said.

Butler hunched his shoulders. Apparently he had walked right into the middle of a personal beef, but he liked being in Masterson and Brown's company, even if it meant ducking some flying lead.

Marshal Singer came over to the table.

"Jim."

"Hello, Fred," Masterson said. "I like your new badge."

Singer looked down at his chest for a moment. To Butler he looked to be in his late thirties, a tall, rangy man.

"I'm sorry, Jim," Singer said. "Somebody had to take the job."

"How does George feel about this, Fred?" Kelley asked. "Or does he even know yet."

"George don't know yet, but I was his deputy a long time. He'll be happy for me."

"Yeah, right," Brown said.

"Jim, I got a job to do," Singer said.

"Then get to it, Marshal," Masterson said, "'cause we got someplace to go."

"Who's this fella?" Singer asked. "And what the hell happened here?"

"A couple of waddies threw down on us, Marshal," Masterson said. "This fella helped us out. As you can see, they got the worst of it."

Singer looked around at the two bodies and the folks stepping around and over them.

"As for who he is, why don't you ask him yourself?" Masterson finished.

Singer looked at Butler and said, "How about it, Mister? Who are you and what's your business here?"

"My name is Butler, Marshal," Butler responded, "and my business is poker."

CHAPTER 10

Butler calmly told the marshal what he had told the others at the table. When it came to the action, all three men supported his story.

"And anybody else in here will tell you the same, Fred," Jim Masterson finished.

"Beggin' your pardon, Jim," Singer said, "but this is your place."

"The people drinkin' and gamblin' in here don't work for me, Fred," Masterson said. "Everythin' happened just the way Mr. Butler told you."

"Well," Singer said, "with you fellas backin' his story, I got to take your word for it. You know these dead fellas, Jim?"

"Never saw them before."

"You think they was hired?"

Neal Brown snorted and asked, "What do you think?"

"By who?"

"That's your job, Marshal," Dog Kelley said, "findin' out who and why, ain't it?"

"You ain't the mayor anymore, Dog," Singer said. "You can't tell me what my job is."

Brown snorted again and said, "Somebody's got to."

"Look," Singer said, facing Neal Brown squarely, "you got a beef with me, Neal? Let's get it out."

Brown started to speak but Masterson said, "Let it lay, Neal. Nobody's got a beef with you, Fred. You're right, somebody had to take the job. I wish you luck with it."

Singer faced Jim Masterson.

"That's real decent of ya, Jim," he said. "I appreciate it. Well, I best get your place cleaned up for ya."

"Appreciate it, Fred," Masterson said, standing. "We're gonna go over to Dog's while you take care of it."

"You stayin' in town, Mr. Butler?"

"I am, Marshal," Butler said, also rising. "I have a room over at the Dodge House."

"Well," Singer said, "I'd appreciate it if ya didn't shoot anybody else while you was in town."

"That ain't fair—" Neal Brown started, but Masterson silenced him with a hand on his arm.

"I can assure you, Marshal," Butler said, "I'll try my very best not to."

"Come on, Butler," Kelley said, "come over to the Alhambra with us. I'll show you some real hospitality."

"Thank you, Mr. Kelley. I'd be honored to."

"It's Dog," Kelley said, "just call me Dog. Everybody does."

They walked together over to the Alhambra, where they sat at a table in the back that was reserved for Dog Kelley and his partner, Pete Beatty. Since Butler had been there just a little while ago another poker game had broken out, and there were now three going on.

"If poker is really your game," Dog Kelley said to him, "this is the place for you."

"I hate to admit it, but he's right," Jim Masterson said, "you'll get better poker here than at my place, especially if you're lookin' for high stakes."

"And real gamblers," Neal Brown said. "That's Ben Thompson over there at that table of five."

"I heard Luke Short is dealing faro over at the Long Branch," Jim Masterson said. "Working for Chalk Beeson and Bill Harris."

"Yeah, but when he wants to play poker he comes here," Kelley pointed out. "You'll get some good games here, Mr. Butler, and I'll extend you all the credit you need."

"Why would you do that, Dog?"

"You helped out my good friend Jim, here," Kelley said. "Kept him from getting' killed on the self-same day he got fired. That's worth a lot to me."

"Even more to me," Masterson admitted. "In fact, Mr. Butler, it's worth a steak at the Delmonico, if you're interested."

"That's actually where I was headed when I stopped into the Lady Gay," Butler admitted.

"Well, finish up your beer, friend," Masterson said. "There's steaks a-waitin'."

Kelley stayed at the Alhambra because it was getting busy. Neal Brown accompanied Masterson and Butler to the Delmonico, where they ordered steak dinners with all the fixin's.

"How long do you figure on stayin' in Dodge, Mr. Butler?" Neal Brown asked.

"Long enough for you to start calling me Ty, I hope."

"Ty?"

"For Tyrone."

"That's a helluva name to hang on a youngster," Jim Masterson said. "You must've had a lot of fights when you were growin' up."

"I had my share," Butler admitted. "You can call me Ty, or Butler. It's your choice."

Masterson thought a moment, then said, "I think I prefer Butler."

"Me too," Brown said. "So, how long *will* you be here, Butler?"

"I don't have a set time," Butler said. "I am moving west, but I'm not in a hurry. I guess it'll depend on how my luck turns."

"Well," Masterson said, "it's gotta get better than it was today."

"Oh, I don't know," Butler said. "I could have taken a bullet."

"True enough," Masterson said. "True enough," but I think you might've got yourself on the wrong side of some people today."

"If they're the kind of people who have other people shot in the back," Butler said, "I think I'm on the right side."

CHAPTER 11

───◆───

After their steaks Jim Masterson was going back to his own place, the Lady Gay. Butler said he thought he'd go to the Alhambra and play some poker.

"Mind if I tag along?" Neal Brown asked. "I'd like to see you in action."

"Be my guest," Butler said.

The three men left the restaurant and walked as far as the Lady Gay together, where Masterson wished them luck and a good night.

When Butler and Brown reentered the Alhambra it was even more crowded and lively. Butler had been tempted to try the Long Branch, but decided to save that until tomorrow.

Once inside, Butler and Brown got themselves a beer each and walked to the back where the poker games were going on. There were still three tables, and no seats open. That was all right with Butler. He wanted to watch the competition for a while.

"Are you sure that's Ben Thompson?" he asked Neal Brown.

"Dead sure. Why?"

Butler shrugged.

"I thought he'd be bigger."

Dog Kelley sidled up alongside them.

"Are you interested in starting another table?" he asked Butler.

"I'd like to watch these for a while."

Kelley nodded and smiled. "It's a wise man who investigates his opponents first. Just let me know what you want, gents. Drinks, cards, a poke with one of the girls."

"On the house?" Neal Brown asked, hopefully.

"For our guest," Kelley said, "not for you, Neal."

"I'm much obliged, Dog," Butler said.

"Just so you know," Dog added to Butler, "the offer of a woman for free is for tonight only."

"I'll keep that in mind," Butler promised.

As Kelley walked away Butler said, "He doesn't seem that upset for someone who just lost an election."

"Dog knows somebody's gotta win and somebody's gotta lose," Brown explained. "He's a politician."

"And what about you fellas?"

"We're not politicians, we're lawman," Brown said. "Jim's upset about bein' fired."

"And you?"

"I'll get me another star somewhere down the road, sooner or later," the ex-deputy said. "But Dodge City, it means something to the Mastersons. They all wore badges here, and Ed died here. Yeah, Jim'll be upset for a while, but he's got some distraction now."

"What's that?"

"Stayin' alive, if tonight's any indication."

"You said you knew who sent those boys after him?"

"Had to be either Al Updegraff, or Peacock."

"Isn't Peacock his partner?"

"Yeah, but they ain't getting' along so good," Brown said.

"And Updegraff?"

"Peacock's brother-in-law. That's part of the problem."

"So because they're having some kind of dispute, they'd have Jim killed?" Butler asked.

"I don't have much knowledge of business," Brown admitted, "but it seems to me, that might be cheaper than buyin' him out."

"What about being bought out?"

"Peacock likes owning the Lady Gay too much," Brown said, "so that ain't gonna happen."

"Well, he's got you to watch his back."

"That didn't do him so much good tonight, did it?" Brown asked. "You saved both our asses."

"I just happened to be in the right place at the right time," Butler said, his eyes on Ben Thompson. The Texan had a reputation with cards and with a gun. Butler wondered if he was as cool with either.

"Don't say that like it's an accident," Neal Brown said. "In my experience, bein' in the right place at the right time is a talent."

"You may be right."

"But you're right about one thing," Brown said. "I do want to watch Jim's back. I got to get back to the Lady Gay. I just wanted to ask you somethin'."

"What's that?" Butler took his eyes off Thompson and looked at Brown.

"The rest of the time you're here," Brown said, "if

you could manage to keep bein' in the right place at the right time I'd be obliged. I'd like to keep Jim alive. He's a good friend of mine."

"I'll do what I can," Butler promised.

"Bat may be in Tombstone," Brown went on, "and maybe they ain't talkin', but I don't wanna have to explain to him why I let another brother get killed in Dodge."

"Can't say I blame you for that."

"Thanks. I'll see you around tomorrow, then?"

"That's where I'll be." When Brown frowned at him he added, "Around, I mean."

"Oh, okay," Brown said. "'night. And good luck."

Butler watched Neal Brown make his way through the crowd and out the batwing door onto the street. Beyond that he couldn't help the man anymore tonight. He turned his attention back to Ben Thompson's poker table, where a man seemed about to get up from his seat.

"Come on, friend," Dog Kelley said, appearing again and clapping him on the back, "I'll get you in there."

CHAPTER 12

There was no house dealer at the table. The games were dealer's choice. The stakes were higher than the other two tables, due to the presence of Ben Thompson. None of those facts deterred Butler. This was his kind of game—the kind he could win or lose a lot of money in.

He introduced himself to all the players, who nodded and muttered their names. Ben Thompson simply nodded, assuming Butler would know who he was. This was either arrogance or Thompson had already sized Butler up as a man who, in turn, sized up his opponents before sitting down.

The other possibility was that he had heard of Butler before.

The game was five handed. Aside from Butler and Thompson, there were Ed Rahy, the town tailor; Harry Kane, who owned and operated the largest livery in town; and Mike Deaver, a local who considered himself a gambler, with a source of money to back him up. There was always one in the game, Butler thought, thinking of Wichita. Hopefully, this one's father was not a banker.

Butler was sitting right across from Thompson. On his left was Rahy, who was dealing. That was good. They'd go completely around the table before he had to deal for the first time. He could watch them each closely while they dealt.

Rahy chose five-card stud, and dealt out the first two cards; one up, one down. Butler followed the cards around the table. Thompson got a four of hearts, Deaver a king of spades, Kane a seven of clubs, he got a jack of diamonds, and the dealer, Rahy, gave himself a ten of spades.

Deaver was the first to act. "Fifty dollars," he said. "Finally got somethin' I can play."

Butler saw a look pass over Thompson's face. He had the feeling the youngest man at the table was bothering him.

"Call," Kane said.

Butler checked his hole card. "Call."

"I call," Rahy said.

"Raise," Thompson said.

"With a four?" Deaver asked. "Come on, Mr. Thompson. You can wait for a better card than that to bluff with."

"I raise a hundred," Thompson said, without looking at or acknowledging Deaver.

"Well, I'll just have to call that raise," Deaver said, and tossed in his money. They were using real money, mostly paper, not chips, so there was only a slight rustling sound.

Kane folded.

"I call," Butler said.

"Now see?" Deaver said. "Him I'm afraid of. He's got a jack."

He seemed to be talking to no one in particular, or to the table at large, but Butler had already figured out that Deaver was needling Thompson, and had probably been doing it all night. He also noticed that Deaver had more money in front of him than any other player. Butler hated when the biggest mouth at the table had the biggest poke.

Rahy, the dealer, folded his ten. That left only Deaver, Thompson, and Butler.

"Pot's right," Rahy said, and dealt the third card.

Thompson got a three of hearts, Deaver a queen of spades, and Butler a ten of diamonds.

"Looks like we're all headed for straight flushes," Deaver said, "but mine'll be a royal, Mr. Thompson, and yours'll just be a little baby straight."

Butler couldn't understand why a young man like Deaver would needle a known man like Thompson, unless it was the younger man's intention to try Thompson, at some point.

"It's your bet, Mike," Rahy said, sounding fatigued, probably from listening to the young man run his mouth all night.

"I'm gonna bet two hundred," Deaver said. "I really like my hand. What about you, partner?" He looked at Butler.

"I believe I'll just call."

Now they all looked at Thompson.

"Raise two hundred."

"Mr. Thompson," Deaver said, shaking his head, "no

offense, sir, but your luck has been so bad all night that I'll just have to call."

"Call," Butler said.

"Pot's right," Rahy said, and dealt the fourth card around. Thompson paired his fours, killing any chance of the baby straight flush Deaver was predicting for him. However, Deaver got a jack of spades, which kept his chances of a royal flush open—except for one thing.

Butler got a ten, giving him a pair of tens and making him high man on the table.

"I'll go a hundred," he said.

"Call," Thompson said right away.

"Now, how come I'm the onliest one you ever raise, Mr. Thompson?" Deaver asked.

"Maybe it's because you got a big mouth, Mike," Rahy said.

"Now you're a dealin', Ed, but otherwise you ain't in this hand, so why don't you shut up?"

Rahy just rolled his eyes.

"Make your play, Deaver," Butler said. "None of us is getting any younger."

"Well, all right then," Deaver said. "Here's your hundred and I raise three. How about that?"

"Call," Butler said.

"I call," Thompson said.

"Oh, now yer just callin'?" Deaver asked, smiling, showing gaps where teeth used to be. Butler wondered if he'd gotten them knocked out in a poker game or two.

"Last card," Rahy said, and dealt them out quickly. Nine of spades for Thompson, no help. Ace of spades for Deaver, who now had the jack, queen, king, and ace.

"Woo-wee," Deaver said, "Lookee that. All I need is the ten—or do I already got it in the hole?"

Butler's last card was an eight of hearts. He was still high man with a pair of tens.

"Two hundred," he said.

"I call," Thompson said, immediately.

"Ain't nobody afraid of my itty-bitty royal flush?" Deaver asked. "Mr. Thompson, with them fours you're likely to keep yer luck runnin' poorly—"

Suddenly, Ben Thompson's gun was in his hand. Rahy and Kane, spectators, pushed their chairs back, as if to jump up and run, but all Thompson did was put his gun down on the table.

"You gonna bet yer gun, Ben?" Deaver asked. "Runnin' short of funds?"

"No," Thompson said, "I'm gonna kill you if you say one more word. Just play your cards, boy. You been runnin' your mouth at me since you sat down. It stops now. Just play your cards and shut the hell up."

"Now, Mr. Thompson, I didn't mean—"

Thompson cocked the pistol and the table fell quiet. Suddenly, people around them noticed the gun and the room quieted as well.

"Play, you pansy fucker, and don't say another word except 'raise' or 'call'."

Butler watched Deaver closely. The younger man bit his lip, eyed Thompson's gun. If he'd been trying to goad Ben Thompson, he certainly didn't want to make his play with Thompson's gun already on the table.

Finally, he made up his mind and pushed all his money into the pot.

"I have three thousand and some dollars here," he said. "I bet it all."

Butler looked into the younger man's glassy eyes and knew he was bluffing. He knew there was no royal flush, but he also knew that both he and Thompson had the boy beat. Deaver was desperate to bluff them out and take their money—especially Thompson's.

"I'm going to have to go into my pocket to call this bet, Ben," Butler said to Thompson. "That all right with you?"

"Go ahead," Thompson said. "I have no beef with you, Butler."

Butler pulled some money from his inside jacket pocket. It was the five thousand he'd gotten from Three-Eyed Jack for the marker the kid had written him. He peeled off three thousand and put the other two back.

"I call," he said, and tossed the money into the pot.

"You call?" Deaver asked, in disbelief.

"Not only don't you have a royal, son," Butler said, "you've got nothing at all."

"H-how do you know that?" Deaver demanded. "I could have a royal."

"No you can't you stupid shit," Rahy said. "I folded your ten of spades. If you'd watch the cards you'd know that."

"Huh?" Deaver thought a moment, then said, "I want my money back."

"Leave it!" Thompson shouted.

By now everybody in the Alhambra was either watching or, if they were too far away or blocked, listening.

"He's right," Thompson said, "we both got you beat.

I've got three fours, but I'm folding because I think Butler has us both beat."

Ben Thompson turned all his cards facedown.

"You're called, Mike," Rahy, the dealer, said. "Whataya got?"

"Huh? Oh, I got ... well ..."

"Just turn the card over," the dealer said.

Deaver did. Butler had been wrong. He did have something. A pair of kings. Still would have made him third in a three-handed pot. Butler turned over his third ten.

"Three tens is the winner," Rahy said.

"Nice hand, Mr, Butler," Thompson said, putting his gun away.

"Thank you, Mr. Thompson." Butler raked in his money.

Mike Deaver sat with a stunned look on his ace. Butler watched him carefully, now that Thompson's gun was off the table.

"You still playing, Mike?" Rahy asked as Ben Thompson gathered the cards for his deal.

"Huh? Oh, uh, no, I'm ... busted."

"Then get the hell up and let somebody else play," Thompson said to him. "Go on ... get!"

Deaver stood up and Butler saw the silver gun with a pearl handle on his hip. The boy was no gunman, just a show off.

As Deaver left and new players sat down, Butler thought it had been a hell of a first hand.

CHAPTER 13

Two hours later Butler was still ahead, most of it on Mike Deaver's money. Since that first hand he'd been playing pretty evenly, while Ben Thompson—his mood improved by Deaver's absence—got hot.

"I'm gonna have a beer and come right back," Butler said, pushing away from the table.

"You can have a beer at the table," Rahy said. "We don't mind."

"Sorry," Butler said, "but I ain't smart enough to do two things at one time like that."

That made Ben Thompson laugh, and he asked, "You mind if I join you for one? These boys can play three-handed for a while ... right boys?"

"Sure, Ben," the other echoed.

Thompson stood up and said to Butler, "Come on, I'll buy."

"Much obliged, Ben."

As they walked to the bar, men moved and formed a path for Ben Thompson and his new friend.

"Two beers," Thompson said when they reached the mile-long Alhambra bar.

"You really don't have to—" Butler started, but Thompson cut him off.

"This is for busting that big-mouthed kid out of the game," he said. "For some reason I just couldn't get it done myself. What you did was a thing of beauty."

"Thanks," Butler said. "He wasn't really that hard to read."

He froze, for a moment wondering if Thompson would take that as an insult.

"I know it," Thompson said. "For some reason he just got my goat running his mouth at me like that. I thought he was trying to push me into a fight, but he had his chance when he stood up. See that fancy piece of his?"

"I saw it," Butler said. "Turns out he was no more a gunman than he was a poker player."

"I guess not."

Their beers arrived and they each drank down half the mug before coming up for air.

"First night in town, or first night playing?" Thompson asked.

"First night in town."

"Staying long?"

"Long enough to make some more money."

"Saw Dog usher you into your seat," Thompson said. "Friend of his?"

"Just met tonight, over at the Lady Gay," Butler said. "There was, uh, some commotion."

"Was that you?" Thompson asked. "I heard somebody kept Jim Masterson from getting shot in the back."

"Yeah, that was me. Right place, right time."

"So you're as good with a gun as you are with a deck of cards?" Thompson asked.

"I get by with both."

"You do more than get by, my friend," the other man said. "You're damned good."

"Thanks. Ben. I appreciate that."

"I appreciate a man who can handle his cards," Thompson said. "You're a slick dealer, too. Not that I'm saying you cheat, don't get me wrong. You just handle the cards real well. I'll bet if you were bottom dealing I'd hardly see it."

"I'll bet if I was bottom dealing," Butler said, "you would have seen it right off and I wouldn't be standing here."

Thompson laughed and slapped Butler on the back.

"Let's finish these drinks and get back to the table. We got some sheep to shear."

The emptied their mugs and retraced their steps back through the path in the crowd to their poker table. The other three didn't look real happy to see them. It seemed the only time one of them had won a hand was just now, while Butler and Thompson were gone.

Butler sat down, thinking his luck was going to change now—and for the better.

CHAPTER 14

———◆———

Butler woke up the next morning with a warm, naked hip pressed against his. He frowned, then remembered that he had finally decided to take Dog Kelley up on his offer for a free woman. He lifted himself up onto his elbows to take a look at her. Her face, in repose, was pretty, and young looking. Her body was long and lean, her skin smooth and clear. Butler figured she wasn't more than twenty-five. He remembered more, that Kelley had given him his choice of any woman, and when he had picked this one, Dog had congratulated him.

"You got the pick of the litter, my friend. Enjoy."

He'd come back to his room in the Dodge House and had done just that, until they were both exhausted, and then they had drifted off to sleep.

He was about to wake her up when he realized he could not remember her name. He recalled most of what had transpired last night—the poker game, apparently making friends with Ben Thompson, picking the girl—but for the life of him he couldn't dredge up her name.

She shifted then, stretched prettily and licked her pretty mouth. As her eyes fluttered open it suddenly came to him in a flash.

"Good morning, Sheila."

She smiled.

"You remembered."

"Of course I remembered," he said. "How could I not after a night like last night."

"You're sweet," she said. She sat up, swung her legs to the floor, then looked over her shoulder at him. She looked very fetching, but his stomach was growling, demanding to be tended to.

"Do you want a morning poke before I go?" she asked.

"Um, if it wouldn't insult you, no," he said. "I really have to get going."

"I'm not offended," she said, standing up. He hadn't noticed last night that her butt was kind of flat, like a boy's. And now that she was standing he could see how small her breasts were. She really wasn't the type of woman he usually liked. He wondered how much he'd had to drink last night? Had he and Ben Thompson gone to the bar again after the game broke up?

She grabbed her dress and slipped into it, then put on her shoes.

"Last night was nice," she said.

"Yeah, it was," he said. "Thanks."

She went to the door, opened it, then turned and wriggled her fingers at him.

"Bye. See you later, maybe."

"Bye, Sheila."

After she left he got up, washed himself using the

pitcher and basin on top of the chest of drawers, then
got dressed, strapped on his gun and went down to have
breakfast.

The steak at the Delmonico had been excellent the night
before but he decided to have breakfast in the Dodge
House's restaurant. When he entered he saw that the
tables were pretty much taken, leading him to believe
that the breakfast there must be pretty good. His stomach grumbled even more as a waiter approached him.

"I'm sorry, sir but—"

"I'm with him," Butler said, pointing.

The waiter turned and saw a man at a table waving
at them.

"Very well, sir," the waiter said. "This way."

Butler followed the waiter to the table, then quickly
asked for coffee, eggs, bacon, and biscuits.

"Coming up, sir."

Butler sat down with the man, who had not yet been
served his breakfast, and said, "Good morning, Mr.
Mayor."

"'Mornin'," Dog Kelley said, "and I ain't Mr. Mayor
anymore, so it's just Dog, like I said last night."

"You eat breakfast here every morning?" Butler
asked.

Kelley nodded. "Start every day here."

Butler looked around. It looked to him as if the other
diners were making a concerted effort not to look at
Kelly.

"Yeah, you're not sittin' with a real popular man in
Dodge," Kelley said. "I can probably get them to bring
another table out for you."

"I don't have a problem with the company I keep," Butler said. "Don't worry about it."

"I'm much obliged," Kelley said. "I usually can't get through breakfast without somebody comin' up to me, askin' me for a favor or just kissin' my ass so I'll make some kind of a decision go their way. I actually don't mind bein' left alone."

Butler didn't much believe that. He had the impression Dog Kelley quite enjoyed being a politician.

The waiter came with his coffee, promised his breakfast very shortly.

"How'd you do last night?" Kelley asked. "Heard from my bartender you sat down with Ben Thompson."

"I did well," Butler said, "but so did Ben."

"Ben? You got on a first-name basis with him?"

"Pretty much," Butler said. Briefly, he told Kelley about the opening hand, and by the time he finished his story the waiter was there with their breakfasts. Kelly's matched Butler's, except for the thick piece of steak that sat in the center of the plate. It was running and turning the eggs pink.

"I like to start the day with a nice rare steak," Kelley explained. He cut off a piece and stuck it in his mouth. "I know the kid you're talkin' about. That pearl-handle gun is a giveaway. His Pa's got a spread outside of town, pretty big one."

"Is he going to run home and tell Daddy we took his money?" Butler asked.

"Maybe, but if he does his Pa will probably smack him," Kelley said. "Big Bob Deaver believes in a man standin' up for himself."

"Well, I think if he'd tried to stand up to Ben Thompson he would've ended up dead."

"No doubt."

"He made the right decision to walk away."

"However," Kelley said, "if I was you I'd watch my back. He may not be as afraid of you as he is of Ben."

"That's just the thing," Butler said around a mouthful of eggs, "he wasn't afraid of Ben at all—at least, not in the beginning. As soon as I sat down I could tell he'd been needling Ben all night."

"Yeah, I heard about the gun on the table, too."

"I guess not much happens in your place without you knowing it, huh?" Butler asked.

"I try to keep track," Kelley said. "It'll probably be easier to run my business, though, now that I don't have to run the town."

Once again Butler could tell the man wasn't happy about the latter.

"You won't take offense if I check out the Long Branch Saloon tonight, will you?" he asked.

"Hell, no," Kelley said. "Chalk's got to make a livin'; like everyone else. Give him my best."

"I will."

"By the way," Kelley asked, "how was Sheila last night?"

"She was fine," Butler said, "just fine."

"Hank told me you took me up on my offer of a free poke."

"I'm afraid we fell asleep, though," Butler said, "so you'll probably have to charge me for the whole night."

Kelley chased some steak and eggs with a mouthful of

coffee, then said, "Forget it. Maybe a night with Sheila will get you to come back for more. Maybe a different girl, next time."

"She was good," Butler said, "she's just not the type I usually pick." He didn't want to admit he couldn't remember picking her. He should not have gotten that drunk the first night in a strange town—certainly not Dodge City.

"We got others," Kelley said, "short, tall, fat, skinny, you name it."

"I'll keep that in mind."

Over the rest of the meal and some more coffee they discussed some town politics, mainly because Butler had made the mistake of asking, "So what do you think of your new mayor?" He was forced to listen to Kelley hold forth on all of Mayor A. B. Webster's shortcomings.

When they were done eating Kelley said, "I'm sorry. I chewed your ear about politics, which you probably ain't interested in."

"Not usually," Butler said, "but this is Dodge City. I'm interested in the history."

"Well," Kelley said, wiping his mouth with a napkin, "if it's history that interests you let me tell you some wild stories about Jim Masterson's brother, Bat ..."

CHAPTER 15

———◆———

Not only did Kelley tell tales of Bat Masterson but Wyatt Earp and his brother as well. They took the conversation outside, where an April breeze raised dust from the dry dirt of Front Street. Butler could see, though, where ruts in the street would fill with water from a good rain. Like most towns, the street would turn to mud when somebody spit.

They grabbed a couple of wooden chairs and sat in front of the hotel, Butler still listening to Kelley's stories.

"So what's going on between Bat and Jim?" Butler asked when the ex-mayor paused for a breath.

"Damned if I know," Kelley said. "Damned if anybody knows. That's between Bat and Jim, and ain't one of them talkin' about it."

"What about this thing between Jim and his partner?"

"Jim made a bad move partnering with A. J. Peacock. The man's a snake, and his brother-in-law ain't much better. I think he's tryin' to force Jim to sell out to him."

"And if he doesn't?"

Kelley shrugged. "That's between Jim and Peacock. I got enough problems getting' along with my own partner."

"Problems there, too?"

"Not the kind that Jim has, no," Kelley said. "Just normal partner problems."

They sat for a few moments in silence, and then Kelley said, "This is very odd."

"What?"

Kelley had been staring out at the street. Now he turned to look directly at Butler.

"Being able to sit here and talk without havin' to worry about going to City Hall."

"It's probably early to think about this," Butler said, "but are you thinking of running again?"

"Hell, yeah," Kelley said fervently. "Wait until this town sees what a mess Webster makes. I'm damn sure gonna run against him next time." Kelley firmed his jaw. "I miss the damn job already."

He stood up, and Butler followed suit.

"Don't listen to me when I say I'm glad to be out of that job," Kelley said. "Politics is in my blood, and it kills me that I ain't mayor anymore." The man fell silent a moment, then repeated, "It kills me."

He stepped down into the street and crossed without another word. Butler didn't even have a chance to thank him for the stories, or for picking up the breakfast check.

The slump of Dog Kelley's shoulders was decidedly sad.

* * *

A. J. Peacock came downstairs from his room and found his brother-in-law, Al Updegraff, sleeping on top of the Lady Gay's bar. He walked over to the snoring man and rolled him off. Updegraff came awake when he hit the floor with a thud, rolled over onto his back.

"Ow," he said, peering up at Peacock. "What'd you do that for?"

"I don't want Masterson comin' down and findin' you on the bar," Peacock said. "That is, unless you're ready to burn powder with him."

"I ain't even awake," Updegraff said, "how'm I supposed to trade lead with Jim Masterson."

"Get up, then," Peacock said, quelling the desire to kick his brother-in-law. "For an ex-lawman, you're a disgrace."

Updegraff climbed to his feet, staggered behind the bar, grabbed a half-full bottle of whiskey and tipped it up, draining it.

"What's your problem?" he asked Peacock, wiping his mouth on his sleeve.

"I've taken sides with you against Masterson, that's my problem," Peacock said.

"You want Masterson's piece of the Lady Gay, that's why yer takin' my side. You think I don't know that?"

"Whatever the reason," Peacock said, "the day may come when you and me have to take matters into our own hands."

"Hey," Updegraff said, "if it wasn't for that tinhorn gambler, Masterson would be dead."

"Yeah, well, let's not forget if we kill Jim we may have to deal with Bat. That's why we can't be the ones who pull the trigger."

"Well, those boys you sent last night sure didn't get the job done," Updegraff muttered.

"Boys I sent?" Peacock asked. "You picked them out, Al!"

"You sent them after him."

Peacock and Updegraff stared at each other, then both looked upstairs, where Jim Masterson's room was. If he'd heard them he would have come out by now.

"Keep your damned voice down," Peacock said. "Look, you find three or four boys who can do the job, understand? Tinhorn gambler or no. And let me know when you get them."

"Yeah, okay."

Updegraff reached for another bottle and Peacock said—still keeping his voice down—"and stop drinkin' my whiskey!"

Butler took a turn around Dodge City, taking in everything, including the not yet open Long Branch Saloon, and the fairly dead red-light district. Nothing in the district opened until late in the day.

Along the way he picked up a copy of the *Dodge City Times*. It was obvious that Mike Deaver's old man was going to find out what had happened to his son in the Alhambra the night before, because it was in the newspaper. There must have been a reporter in the Lady Gay, observing everything, because the story was very accurate. So accurate, in fact, that it mentioned everyone at the table—including him.

He folded the paper and shook his head. This wasn't good, but then who back East read the *Dodge City Times*? And it wasn't as if they weren't going to find him again. They were. They would always find him and try him. He supposed that one day he'd get tired of it and return to the East, but this wasn't that day.

He stood on the corner of Front and 2nd Avenue. It was nearing lunchtime and the town had come to life long ago. Wagons and horses moving up and down Front Street, men and women passing him on the street, some bidding him good morning or good day, others nodding, still others ignoring. He was wearing a dark suit, boiled white shirt, and string tie, along with his good boots. It was the way he usually dressed, and pretty much branded him a gambler, but he liked the way he looked when he dressed this way. And he never tried to hide his profession from anyone.

He'd spotted a small café during his walk, and decided it was a likely place for lunch. He'd sniffed the aromas coming from inside, recognized the smell of baking. He was in the mood for coffee and pie.

CHAPTER 16

The café was small and filled with delicious smells. Even after the full breakfast he'd had, his mouth started to water when he walked in. There were only a few tables—mismatched, and they looked handmade, as did the chairs—and none of them were taken, at the moment. He looked around, waited and when no one appeared, he seated himself. After a few moments he called out, "Anybody home?"

Abruptly, a man stuck his head in from what Butler assumed was a curtained doorway to the kitchen.

"Oh, sorry," he said, "didn't hear you come in." He came out the door, cleaning his hands on the once white apron he wore around his ample waist. "Fact, is, hardly nobody ever comes in here."

"I don't see why not?" Butler asked. "There sure are good smells coming from here."

"Obliged to you for that, Mister," the man said. "You must be a stranger in town. See, most local folks eat over to the Delmonico, or in one of the hotels. I keep stuff on the stove just in case, but most of the time me and my family ends up eatin' it ourselves."

"Well, I wouldn't want to deprive your family of anything—" Butler started to say.

"No, hey," the man said, "I'm in business, after all. What's your pleasure? I got some real good beef stew on the stove."

His intention had been to only have some pie, but now he felt he needed to order something more.

"Sounds good," Butler said. "I'll try a bowl of that, and follow it with some pie."

"Somethin' ta drink for ya?"

"Coffee."

"Comin' up," the man said, turning toward the kitchen. He stopped before entering, though, turned back. "You are gonna be here when I come back out, right?"

"I'm going to be right here waiting for that beef stew," Butler said.

The man smiled and went through the curtain. Butler wondered how many folks had come in, ordered something and left before he came out. And why?

After he'd eaten two bowls of beef stew, a piece of apple pie, and drank a pot of coffee, Butler was even more confused about why someone would leave the café before eating.

The cook—who was also the owner and the waiter, a fellow named Hank—came out and asked him if he wanted anything else.

"I can't eat another thing," Butler said. He was glad he hadn't put on a vest today. He'd have popped the buttons by now. "That was a fine meal, Hank."

"Well, thank ya. I appreciate that... hell, I didn't even ask you your name. I got the manners of a goat."

"My name's Butler, Ty Butler." The gambler stood up to shake the cook's hand.

"Well, hey—you're the fella saved Jim Masterson's bacon last night in the Lady Gay."

"I guess you could say that."

"And busted young Mike Deaver out of a poker game."

Butler would've said word got around fast, but he still had that copy of the *Times* with the story in it. He knew he couldn't have been the only one who read it.

"Looks like I made quite a name for myself my first day in town," Butler said. "And I usually try to keep a low profile."

"Well, I'm just pleased to make your acquaintance, Mr. Butler," Hank said. "Any friend of the Mastersons is a friend of mine, yes sir. Real damn glad to meet ya."

"You know all of them?" Butler asked, retrieving his hand before the man could crush it.

"Fact is, I got a passin' acquaintance with Jim," Hank said, "but I respect him as a lawman. He was a good one for years, here. I don't know Bat, but I knew Ed before he got killed. That goes back a ways, when I was still a blacksmith."

"Wait, wait ... you went from being a blacksmith to a cook?" That explained the size of the man, who must've stood six two with a belly like a boulder.

"Sounds funny, I know, but I always preferred cooking. I saved up enough money to open this place. Only been here a few months. Tell ya the truth, don't know how much longer I can last, but it's sure gratifying to know you liked my cooking."

"I think that was the best meal I've had in a while," Butler said, "and I had a steak at the Delmonico last night."

"Well, then, I am much obliged to ya," Hank said.

"I'll spread the word, Hank," Butler said. "Maybe I can send some business your way."

"I'd sure appreciate that, Mr. Butler," Hank said. "I sure would."

Butler nodded and worked his way to the door. He wanted to get out before Hank decided to shake hands again.

CHAPTER 17

❖

Butler had not meant to become so infamous in Dodge City. His intention had been to simply come there and play poker. It's all he ever wanted to do when he came to a town. Fact of the matter was most of his trouble—that which didn't come from the East—came because he could not mind his own damned business.

And he couldn't very well have stood by and watched Jim Masterson get shot in the back. He hated back shooters, had managed to avoid a couple of them himself. He respected men who came straight at him to try to kill him, but when they came from behind they deserved no less than what they themselves were trying to dole out.

As he walked through town earlier, heading toward the Dodge House, he'd guessed that some of the folks who saw him on the street had probably not yet read the newspaper. Now it was afternoon, and he felt he was being recognized more often, likely from the article. Suddenly, he noticed that he was right across the street from the office of the *Dodge City Times*, and he decided to go in.

When he entered he smelled ink and oil in the air, both coming from the silent press. There was another room; he saw a man and a woman in there, involved in what appeared to be a heated discussion. That was just as well. He wasn't even sure why he was there and what he wanted to say, yet. Let them finish their argument first.

He waited a good ten minutes, and when he realized the argument was nowhere near being completed he stepped forward and knocked on the door. Both of the people inside turned and looked at him through the glass. They both looked like they were in their twenties, and the resemblance was too close for them to be husband and wife. He put his money on brother and sister.

The man moved first, coming to the door and opening it.

"Yes?"

"I'd like to speak to the editor of the paper, please."

"That's me," both of them said, and then glared at each other.

"Okay," the man said, "we're both editors, and reporters."

"For now," she said, "and only because I don't want to argue in front of this gentleman"—she took a good look at Butler and added—"who, if I'm not mistaken, is Mr. Butler."

"Butler?" the young man said, taking one step back.

"Oh, take it easy, Lou," she said. "He's not a killer, he's a gambler."

"He killed a man last night," Lou pointed out.

Butler decided that the woman was the older of the two, but probably only by a few years.

"She's right, Lou," Butler said. "I'm a gambler."

"Why don't you check the press, Lou?" she suggested. "I'll talk to Mr. Butler."

"Yeah, well, why not?" Lou asked. "You wrote the damned story." He looked at Butler. "Mister, my sister thinks it okay to invade people's privacy just because we run a newspaper. You tell 'er."

With that Lou left, pulling the door closed behind him.

"So that's Lou," Butler said. "And you are?"

"Is that my paper in your coat pocket, there?" she asked.

"Yes, it is."

"Well, my brother's right," she told him. "I wrote the story about you."

Butler pulled the paper out and opened it.

"Says here the writer was somebody named ... M. J. Healy."

"That's me," she said. "Mary Jane Healy. What can I do for you, Mr. Butler? Did I print anything that wasn't true?"

Mary Jane Healy about twenty-eight, tall, well built, her blond hair pulled into a ponytail and tied with a black ribbon, or something.

"Nothing untrue, Miss Healy," he said, "just some truth that might get me killed."

"Killed? Isn't that a little melodramatic? Thinking people are out to kill you?"

If she only knew, he thought.

"Ma'am—" he said.

"Oh God," she said, putting her hands to the sides of her face.

"What is it?"

"Do I look like a Ma'am, now?" she asked. "Has it been that long since a good bar of soap?"

Butler paused and looked at her. She was trying to put him off balance, fishing for a compliment.

"Miss Healy," he said, "I really would rather you didn't write about me in your paper anymore."

"You're a very well-spoken, polite man, Mr. Butler," she said. "Are you from the East?"

"Are you trying to interview me, Miss Healy?"

"M.J., please," she said.

"All right, M.J."

"And would you be willing to be interviewed?"

"No."

"Why not?"

"Because it's bad enough that you wrote about me in one issue, I don't need to be in two."

"Editions."

"What?"

"We call them editions, not issues."

"Whatever you call them," he said. He grabbed her hand and slapped his copy of the paper into it. "I don't want to be in another one. Understand ... Ma'am?"

As he turned and walked he heard her laugh, and say, "Now that was just mean."

Damn it, I like her, he thought.

CHAPTER 18

For want of something better to do, Butler returned to his hotel room. The saloons were open and he could have gone to the Long Branch, but he decided to put that off until later. He had some thinking to do, and he couldn't do it around people—especially not around people who were staring at him.

It was the newspaper story that was causing him problems. Maybe nobody back East read the *Dodge City Times,* but everybody in Dodge read it and now knew who he was. The word could spread, and since an attempt had already been made on him in Wichita, he figured the word would only have to travel about that far.

He could pack up now and leave, head for Tombstone, where the sheer number of known men—the Earps, Bat Masterson, Doc Holliday, Johnny Ringo—would keep him in the background.

Or he could stay here as long as he had intended because Dodge City interested him—even more so now that he knew Jim Masterson, Neil Brown, and Ben Thompson. Being around them could be dangerous, but also would make sure he was never bored in Dodge. Also, if an attempt were made on him, he'd have some back up. And he knew both Brown and Masterson would be with him because of what he'd done in the Lady Gay the night before. Thompson might back his play simply because he liked him.

He walked to the window and looked down at Front Street, busier now with pedestrian and street traffic than at any time of the day. If he was going to remain in Dodge, it was time to be out there.

He'd surprised himself. It hadn't taken him all that long to come to a decision.

When he got to the lobby, he was startled to see the newspaper lady, Mary Jane Healy standing there.

"Good afternoon, Mr. Butler." She greeted him with a broad smile that lit up her face.

"Miss Healy."

"M.J., please."

"Are you down here waiting for me?"

"Yes, I am."

"I thought I made it clear I didn't want to be interviewed."

"I thought I'd make another plea."

"Well, can you make it walking?" he asked.

"I believe I can."

Outside he turned in the direction of the Long Branch, and she stayed with him. She was tall enough to take long enough strides to keep up with him while he walked.

"Tell me, M.J.," he asked, "why would I change my mind now? What's different from twenty minutes ago?"

"Oh, I don't know," she said. "Your attitude? Maybe you've had time to think it over? Maybe I'll just be more persuasive?"

"And how would you do that?"

"I could throw in some incentive?"

He looked at her, but did not slow his pace.

"What kind of incentive."

She grabbed his arm to stop him.

"You know, you're not a very tall man, but you take long strides. Can we stop a minute?"

"Sure."

They were in front of a cigar store, only one or two storefronts from the Long Branch.

"I'm sorry if my writing about you in today's edition has caused you any problems," she said.

"It hasn't."

She opened her mouth to continue, then closed it when she realized what he'd said.

"It hasn't?"

"No," he said, "but it might, in the future. And it's not that I'm so well known I don't want people reading about me. It's just the opposite."

"You don't want to be well known?"

"No," he said, "I don't."

"That makes you a rare man," she said. "Most men want a reputation."

"Well, I don't."

"Why?" she asked curiously. "Are you running from something?"

"I'm not wanted, if that's what you mean."

"That," she said, "or anything else. Is there a wife you left behind who'd like to find you? Someone you owe money to? Or an old enemy?"

"Miss Healy," he said, deliberately, "this is beginning to sound suspiciously like an interview."

"It can't be an interview."

"Why not?"

"I don't have a pad," she said. "When I don't have something to write on, I can't do an interview. This is just me being nosy."

"Well," he said, "I don't answer nosy questions, either."

He started to walk again, so quickly that it took her a few strides to catch up.

"Where are we going?"

"We are not going anywhere," he said. "I'm going to the Long Branch Saloon."

"Good," she said. "I could use an afternoon drink."

"Miss Healy—"

"I'll buy," she said. "Not as an incentive, just to be nice. Whataya say?"

They were in front of the Long Branch's batwing doors, so he stopped and turned to her.

"All right," he said, finally, "one drink."

CHAPTER 19

Just inside the batwing doors, Butler and M.J. were stopped by a tall, slender man with a large moustache.

"Now, come on, M.J.," he said, the two obviously well acquainted, "you know Chalk don't like you comin' in here."

"Chalk's not here, is he, Bill?" she asked.

"Well, no, he's away with his cowboy band," Bill Harris said. "They're playin' at the capital."

"Bill Harris, this is Tyrone Butler," she said. "I was bringing him here to show him the best place to gamble."

"Butler?" Harris asked. "The fella who busted young Master Deaver out of the game last night?"

"That's me," Butler said, frowning. "But she's not bringing me in here, Mr. Harris. I was on my way here, anyway."

The two men shook hands and Harris said, "Oh, I know that, sir. Our M.J., here, is an accomplished little liar when she's trying to get what she wants. You're welcome in the Long Branch, Mr. Butler," Harris went on, then looked at Mary Jane Healy and added, "but you are not, little lady. We've told you before, you want to write about what goes on in here, send your brother."

"If my brother came in here he'd get too involved with the whiskey, the women, and the cards to write anything," she complained.

"Don't complain to me about your family, M.J.," Harris said. "I got my own to worry about. Now shoo."

"But Butler and I were gonna—"

"Shoo, I said," Harris repeated. "Whatever you and Mr. Butler were going to do, do it later and somewhere else."

He took her by the arm and purposefully—not forcefully, walked her outside.

"I'm sorry about that," he said, when he reentered. "Come on in. Let me buy you a drink and show you around."

Harris walked Butler to the bar—easily as long as the one in the Alhambra, maybe longer—and waved a bartender over.

"Beer," Butler said.

"How long has she been bothering you?" Harris asked Butler.

"I didn't even know she was bothering me until I read the newspaper today."

"Yes, I read that article," Harris said. "I have to admit it was interesting reading. I also wonder who it was gave her the story? I'm sure she wasn't in the Alhambra last night."

"No, I would have noticed her."

"And she's right about her brother," Harris said. "He loses all his focus as soon as he comes into a saloon."

"Lots of men do."

Harris laughed. "I'm sure those are the men you like to take money off of in poker."

Butler turned to face Harris, beer in hand.

"I prefer to take money from men who are alert and know what they're doing. There's sport in that."

"I'm sorry," Harris said, putting his hands up in front of him, palms out. "I didn't mean any disrespect. You'll have to excuse me, but it's my partner Chalk who usually, uh, deals with the public."

"Chalk?"

"Chalky Beeson," Harris said. "He won't even tell me how he got that name. He and I have been partners for some time now."

"And you get along?"

"Famously," Harris said. "You see, we know each other's strengths."

"You're from the East?" Butler asked.

"New Jersey." W.H. Harris had come west from Long Branch, New Jersey, so when he and Chalk Beeson became partners in a saloon he called it the Long Branch.

"I can hear it."

"And you? New York?"

"Philadelphia."

"Close enough," Harris said. "Well, would you like me to show you the games—"

"I don't want to take up any more of your time, Mr. Harris," Butler said. "I think I'll just look around at my own leisure."

"Very well," Harris said. "If there's anything I can do for you, don't hesitate to ask. We'd like you to do your gambling here."

"What about Ben Thompson? Does he play here?"

"Very often," Harris said, "but Ben likes to move around. On any given night you might find him here, the Lady Gay or, as you did last night, the Alhambra."

"Any other gamblers of note in town?" Butler asked.

Harris worked an ear with the tip of his little finger. "I heard some talk of Luke Short coming into town, but I haven't seen him."

"Okay, thanks."

"If you like to cross swords with the best," Harris said, "I can probably set up a private game upstairs."

"Thanks for the offer," Butler said. "I'll let you know."

Harris turned to the bartender. One more on the house and then he pays." He looked at Butler.

"That's fair," the gambler said.

Harris nodded, turned, and walked away. He went through a door in the back of the place, which Butler assumed was an office.

"Want that second one?" the bartender asked.

"When I do," Butler said, "I'll wave."

The bartender nodded, said, "That's fair," and went off down the bar.

CHAPTER 20

Al Updegraff was across the deadline to the red-light district, at a small saloon that served warm beer, worn-out whores, and crooked games. It was the perfect place to find the men he wanted.

He was standing at the bar, wondering what was floating on top of the beer he'd ordered, when three men entered and came up to the bar. He recognized one of them and, based on who he was, decided that he could use all three.

Red Sandland was a somtime customer at the Lady Gay and had been served beer more than once by Updegraff. Real beer, not the swill they served here.

"Hey, Red," Updegraff said.

Sandland looked over at him, frowned, then brightened when he recognized him.

"Jesus Christ, Al," he said, "I didn't recognize you on this side of the bar."

Updegraff shook hands with the man, was introduced to the other two—Dave and Willy—and offered to buy all three men a drink.

"Okay," Sandland said, "but whiskey, not that crap they serve in place of beer. If I want a beer I'll come over to the Lady Gay, right?"

"What are you doin' here?" Updegraff asked, after giving the bartender the order.

"Ah, there's a whore here gives Willy a discount. We're gonna see if she'll take all three of us. What're you doin' here?"

"I'm lookin' for three men who want to make some money," Updegraff said.

"Is that a fact?" Sandland asked. "Would we do?"

"I don't know." Updegraff picked up the bottle of whiskey the bartender had set down and poured each man a drink. "Why don't we discuss it?"

An hour later Updegraff entered the Lady Gay and found his brother-in-law behind the bar counting bottles of whiskey.

"I didn't steal any, if that's what you're worried about," he said testily.

Peacock turned and looked at him.

"I'm takin' inventory, you ass. Did you, uh, take care of that matter we were discussing?"

"Give me a cold beer and I'll tell you," Updegraff said. "I gotta wash the foul taste out of my mouth first."

Peacock drew Updegraff half a mug of beer and pushed it over to him.

Updegraff thought about arguing, then thought better of it. He picked up the beer and drained it, then briefly told Peacock about his conversation with Red Sandland and his two partners.

"And they'll do it?" Peacock asked his brother-in-law.

"They'll do anythin' for money."

"Yeah, but Al, will they do it right?"

"For that," Updegraff said, "you'd have to pay a lot more money than you gave me."

Peacock narrowed his eyes and stared at Updegraff suspiciously.

"Did you give them all of the money I gave you?"

"Sure I did," Updegraff said, "what do you take me for?"

Peacock shook his head. "If you weren't my sister's husband," he said, "I'd take you for dead."

Updegraff, an ex-lawman himself, stood up straight and glared at Peacock. "You don't wanna be talkin' to me that way, Anthony."

Peacock adopted the same stance and the two men stared for a good minute, both wearing guns.

"Have another beer, Al," Peacock finally said.

"A whole one?"

"Yeah," Peacock said, "a whole one."

His sister would never forgive him if he killed Updegraff, and he hoped the same would be true were it the other way around.

Jim Masterson came out of the back office as Updegraff and Peacock were staring each other down. He stood and watched, hoping the two would go for their guns and solve his problems for him—at least some of them. If Peacock killed Updegraff, he wouldn't have to put up with the drunken fool anymore. If it happened the other way around, he wouldn't have to try to figure out what to do about his partnership with Peacock. The man wanted to buy him out, but Masterson didn't want to do that, especially since he'd lost his job as city marshal. And he didn't have the money to buy Peacock out.

He waited, hoping that guns would clear leather, but in the end Peacock gave Updegraff a beer, which the other man downed quickly before taking his leave.

Masterson walked up to Peacock and asked, "What was that all about?"

Peacock looked around quickly, wondered how much his partner had seen or heard?

"Family business," he said.

"It looked pretty serious," Masterson said, "Thought you two were gonna come to blows."

"Yeah, you'd like that, wouldn't ya, Jim? Maybe get rid of one of us that way?"

"Now, Anthony," Masterson asked, "Why would I want to get rid of you?"

Peacock laughed and asked, "Drink?"

"Why not."

"Whiskey?"

Masterson nodded. Peacock poured them each a glass.

"Don't suppose you've given any more thought to my offer?" Peacock asked.

"I ain't interested in selling, A.J.," Masterson said.

"Figured since you weren't marshal anymore, you might want to be movin' on?"

"You figured wrong."

The two men downed their drinks and Peacock replaced the bottle behind the bar.

"Well," he said, "I still got work to do, inventory's got to be took."

"I could do that."

"Really, Jim?" Peacock asked. "You even know how?"

"Well, no, but—"

"Then I'll see you later."

Masterson watched Peacock walk across the saloon to the back room, then got behind the bar himself and started counting whiskey bottles.

CHAPTER 21

————————◆———————

Butler found Mary Jane Healy waiting for him when he left the Long Branch. This time he was not surprised.

"You're persistent," he said.

"Yes, I am," she said. "That's what makes me a good newspaperwoman."

"I don't doubt it," he said.

"Then talk to me," she said, falling into step with him.

"There's nothing to talk about."

"Yes, there is," she said. "Why you're in Dodge, how long you plan to stay—"

"What makes you think your readers would be interested in me?" he asked. "Why not interview somebody like ... Ben Thompson?"

"I did," she said, "when he first came to town. Now *he* was very cooperative."

"He was?"

"Very," she said, nodding.

"When was that?"

"A couple of weeks ago."

"Have you got a copy of that issue?" he asked.

"Of course," she said. "We have copies of every issue—plus issues of other newspapers."

Struck by an idea, he stopped walking. She had to stop abruptly and still went two steps past him.

"I'll make you a deal," he said.

"What?"

"Let me look through your archives and I'll let you interview me."

"Our archives? Why?"

"I'm a student of history," he told her. "I want to read up on Dodge City."

"Fine," she said quickly. "I can even help you, save you time having to find specifics about Dodge. I'll just show you the newspapers that will have what you want."

"Okay," he said, "let's go."

"Now?"

"Yes, now," he said. "I've got nothing else to do."

"But ... what about gambling?" she asked. "Don't you want to play poker?"

"I will," he said, "later. Right now I want to see all those newspapers."

"Well," she said, "okay, then, let's go."

When Mary Jane came walking back into the office of the *Dodge City Times* with Butler, her brother raised his eyebrows. He spoke to Butler, not to her.

"I thought you would have lost her by now."

"She's hard to lose," Butler said.

"I know."

"Lou," M.J. said, "Mr. Butler is going to be in the back room looking at old newspapers."

"Fine by me," Lou Healy said, "Just don't breathe too heavy, you'll end up with black ink on your lungs."

Butler looked at M.J.

"He's kidding," she said. "Come on, I'll get you situated and start bringing out some papers."

He followed her into a back room where she left him seated at a long wooden table, then went to get some papers. When she returned she had copies of not only the *Times* but the *Hays Sentinel*, the *Yates Center News*, and even the *New York Herald*.

"When you're finished with these I can get you some more," she said.

"I appreciate it, Miss—"

"Just call me M.J.," she said. "Everybody does."

As she leaned over him he smelled not newspaper ink, but her. She'd obviously had a bath that morning, and her hair smelled fresh and clean. Suddenly, he felt dirty.

"I'll be back to check on you later," she said.

"I'll be here."

At the door she stopped and turned.

"By the way, when can we do that interview?"

"How about tonight?"

She looked surprised.

"That'd be great. I can come to your hotel—"

"Why don't we have supper?" he asked.

"Supper? Oh, you mean ... together? I, uh, usually I eat with my brother but—"

"I'll buy."

"Well ... all right. I guess he can fend for himself tonight," she agreed.

"I'll pick the restaurant," he said. "I know just the place for it. What time do you finish here?"

"About five, but—"

"Let's do it at six, then," he said. "You can conduct the interview while we eat."

"I'll remember to bring a pad," she said. "Well, all right, now that that's settled, I'll leave you to it."

He started going through newspaper, hoping he'd have time to go back to his hotel and have a bath.

CHAPTER 22

Butler read in the *Dodge City Times* that James H. "Dog" Kelley was supposedly the leader of a group called the Dodge City Gang, who wanted Dodge City to be a wide-open town because it was profitable for them that way. Most of them—even lawmen like Wyatt Earp and Jim Masterson—owned saloons and gambling halls.

On the other side were men like A. B. Webster, members of a group called the Reformers. They were determined to clean the town up. They wanted newspapers all over the country to stop printing things like, "The town is full of prostitutes and every house is a brothel" (*Hays Sentinel*); and "Dodge City. A Den of Thieves and Cutthroats—The Whole Town in League to Rob the Unwary Stranger (*Yates Center News*). And even after Prohibition laws were approved in Kansas, the *New York Herald* wrote: "saloons, gambling rooms and dance halls run with perfect freedom and their proprietors are the leading men in town."

The first step toward the Reformers' plan came when

Bat Masterson was narrowly beaten in the election for sheriff by George W. Hinkle. But while Hinkle was thought to be anti-Gang he was also a saloon owner. So it wasn't until just a few days ago, when A. B. Webster defeated Dog Kelley for mayor—after Kelley had served from 1877–1881—that the Reformers really came to power. Hinkle immediately dismissed all of the law enforcement officials and replaced them. That was where the town stood now.

When M.J. came back in Butler took his father's watch out and looked at the time. The pocket watch was the only thing with any sentimental value that he had brought with him when he left home. He was surprised to see that it was almost five.

"I'm sorry," she said. "I got busy and forgot you were back here. Did you find what you wanted?"

"Yes, I did. Thanks." Actually, he'd read all about Dodge City, but he'd never gotten to read the interview she did with Ben Thompson. "Can I help you put these papers back?"

"No, that's okay," she said. "I'll have Lou do it tomorrow. I have to go home and get ready for our interview."

He showed her his black-ink stained fingertips and said, "I have to go back to my hotel and get cleaned up."

"I'll just lock up, then, and we can meet at the restaurant."

He followed her out, and after she'd locked the door he saw her turn and look at him expectantly.

"Are we going to the Delmonico? I can meet you—"

"No," he said, "I'm taking you someplace else."

"I thought we'd meet—"

"I'll come by your home and fetch you," he said. "Just give me directions."

She hesitated only a moment, then complied, giving him detailed instructions on how to reach the house she shared with her brother.

"It's the house we grew up in," she ended.

"You don't have to justify where you live to me," he told her. "I'll see you at six."

Butler was thinking about M.J. Healy as he entered the Dodge House and started up the stairs to the second floor. He reached his room and was about to fit his key into the lock when the door to the room directly across from him opened and a man stepped out.

"Oh, hi," the man said.

Butler was suspicious. The man wasn't dressed like someone who could afford a room at the Dodge House.

"Yeah, hi."

The man closed his own door and stood there a moment, facing the door, his back to Butler, who decided not to move. If the man was waiting for him to open the door to his own room, he was going to have a long wait.

CHAPTER 23

———◆———

Butler's big advantage over most men at the poker table was his patience. He could wait forever for the right moment to make his big bet, the one that would win him that one hand of the night that would make or break him. The same patience usually extended to his real life, as well, and this was one of those times.

The man at the door had no patience. When he realized Butler hadn't yet opened his door he turned, and was startled to find Butler looking right at him.

"Huh?" The sound came from him unbidden, and he couldn't push it back down.

"Walk away, friend," Butler said. "Whatever you've got planned for tonight isn't worth it."

The man's eyes darted left and right. Was he looking for help? Did he have help waiting, perhaps for his signal?

Butler pushed back the flap of his jacket and laid his hand on his gun butt.

"What's it gong to be?"

The man wet his lips, let his eyes dart about again,

then shrugged and said, "I—I don't know what yer talkin' about. I—I got things to do tonight."

"Then go and do them."

The man hesitated, as if unsure which way to go, then turned and went down the hall to the stairway. Butler turned, quickly unlocked his door and entered, closing it firmly behind him. He stood there for a moment, his ear to the door, listening. When he was satisfied there was no movement outside he removed his hand from his gun, and moved away from the door. He went to the window and looked down at Front Street. He was waiting for the man to appear on the street, but it didn't happen. He was either still in the hotel, or he'd left and had remained on this side of the street, where Butler could not see him.

Butler backed away from the window, removed his jacket and hung it on the back of the only chair in the room. He now had neither the time nor the inclination to take a bath. He'd clean himself up best he could for his supper with M.J. The last thing he wanted was to be caught naked in a bathtub, just in case the fellow was coming back with friends.

He kept his gun on while he washed.

When Sandland reached the stairs his two compadres, Dave and Willy, were there, standing just below the top step.

"What happened?" Willy asked.

"Did we miss the signal?" Dave asked.

"I didn't give the signal," Sandland said. "The sonofabitch wouldn't go into his room—and then he braced me."

"Why didn't you—"

"Let's go down to the lobby," Sandland said. "I don't wanna talk up here."

The three men went down the stairs, but then Sandland decided they shouldn't talk in the lobby, either.

"Let's go get a drink," he said.

"What about the gambler?" Dave asked.

"We'll take care of him later."

"Let's go to the Lady Gay," Willy said.

"No!" Sandland said quickly. He didn't want to have to explain to Al Updegraff why they hadn't taken care of the gambler yet. "No, the Red Dog is just down the street. We'll go there. I don't want to get too far from the hotel, in case the guy comes out again."

"But what about—"

"Just shut up, Willy," Sandland said. "Just shut up for now."

"You're havin' supper with this man?" Lou Healy asked his sister. "You don't even know him?"

"That's the point of the supper, Lou," she said. "To get to know him. To interview him."

"What's he done that makes him worth an interview?" her brother demanded.

"Well, for one thing he's apparently friends with Ben Thompson."

"They just met last night."

"And already they've played cards together and drank together," she said. "Now, I don't much understand men, but that sounds like a new friendship to me. Throw in a whore and they'd be best friends! Isn't that what you men do?"

Lou wasn't hearing her.

"What am I supposed to do about eatin'?" he asked.

"We have some fried chicken left over from the other night," she said, "or go to a restaurant and eat. Go to the Delmonico."

"That's expensive."

"Look, Lou," she said, "he's going to be here any minute. Get all of this out of your system, all right? So you don't look like a big baby in front of him."

She straightened her dress and left him standing there in her bedroom, in front of her mirror. He looked at his own reflection, then muttered after her, "You're a baby."

CHAPTER 24

Butler was extra careful when leaving his room, and when he went down to the lobby. He considered going out a back door, but then decided to brave the front. They'd already tried once to get him in the hallway, maybe they weren't willing to try in the street.

As he left the hotel he realized the coast was clear and started walking toward the far end of town, following M.J.'s directions. As he went he wondered at the fact that somebody was trying to collect the price on his head again so soon after Wichita. He could usually count on weeks, sometimes months, between tries. He also wondered if he should call this supper off. M.J. might be in danger being around him, but then he doubted he'd be able to talk her out of it. She'd already impressed him with her tenacity. She'd probably hound him all night, and be in the line of fire, anyway, if something came up. Better to eat with her, give her the interview, and then send her home where she'd be safe.

He reached the house, a small, one-story wooden building that needed some work. The yard was in disrepair, as was the white fence that went halfway around. He mounted the front steps. Three of them, the middle one loose. This place needed a man with a hammer and some nails, and a good coat of paint.

He knocked on the door and she immediately opened it. She was wearing a smile and a pretty blue dress that showed off her figure without showing him any skin. He liked it better than if she'd been wearing a saloon girl's dress.

"You look beautiful," he said.

"Thank you." She stepped outside and closed the door.

"Not saying goodbye to your brother?"

"We've already said good night," she told him. "He's a little peeved that I'm not cooking dinner."

"Will he starve?"

"I doubt it,"

"That's good."

"Why?" she asked. "If I'd said yes, would you have invited him to come along?"

"No," he said, "I just don't want to be the cause of him starving to death."

"No danger of that."

He extended his arm and asked, "Shall we go?"

She was holding a pad and pencil, so she shifted them to her other hand so she could take his arm.

"Since I don't know where we're going," she said, "I'm on your hands."

He was sure he hadn't been followed to her house, and he was equally sure no one was following them as he walked her to the restaurant he'd discovered, owned and operated by Hank ... whose last name he did not know.

"What is this place?" she asked, when they reached it.

"You've never been here?"

"I didn't even know it existed," she said. "How in the name of heaven did you find it?"

"I just took a walk yesterday, and here it was. I tried the food and it's great."

"Have you been to the Delmonico?"

"This is better."

She looked at him is disbelief. "Really?"

"Really."

"Well," she said, "this I have to see."

"But I want you to do something for me, before we go in," he said.

"Does the interview depend on this, too?"

"No, no," he said, "I've already agreed to do the interview. This is a favor."

"And what is this favor?"

"If you like the food here," Butler said. "You'll write the place up in your newspaper, tell people it's here. You'll recommend it. Will you do that for me?"

She frowned at him.

"Do you own a piece of this place?"

"Not at all," he answered. "Like I told you, I just discovered it yesterday by accident."

"And you liked the food that much?"

"I did."

She looked at the place, the small, dirty front window, narrow doorway, and, inside, the few tables and chairs. She wasn't looking at it with distaste, though. If she had he might have been forced to point out the condition

of her home. No, she was just eyeing the place with ...
curiosity.

"What do you say?" he asked, extending his arm
again.

"Okay," she said, linking her arm in his, "it's a
deal."

They stepped inside.

Hank was thrilled to see Butler back, and even more
thrilled that he had brought a lady with him—and such
a beautiful one. Butler didn't bother to tell the man that
she was also owner of the *Dodge City Times*. He decided to save that for later.

"I'll make you both the best meal you ever had," he
said proudly.

"I'd like a steak, please," she said, and proceeded to
tell him how she wanted it cooked and what she wanted
with it. Butler knew she was doing this so that she could
compare it to the Delmonico, which was famous for its
steaks.

"And you, sir?" Hank asked.

"I'll have the same, Hank, and some coffee."

"Something to drink for the pretty lady?"

"Do you have beer?"

"Ice-cold beer," he said.

"Then that's what I'll have."

"In that case," Butler said, "bring me the same."

Hank actually rubbed his two big hands together as
he said, "It'll be my pleasure."

M.J. looked around the empty place and said, "Looks
like I'm not the only one who doesn't know this place
is here."

"Well," Butler said, "hopefully, after tonight, that will all change."

"Let's see how I like the steak, first, shall we?"

"Don't worry," he assured her. "You'll like it."

"Why don't we start the interview?" she asked. "I mean, while we have the time?"

He looked down at her pad and pencil on the table and said, "I'm ready when you are."

CHAPTER 25

She started out asking him some easy questions: How he got started playing poker, some of the famous people he's played with, his most difficult game. She continued to ask and he to answer throughout dinner and dessert, and then it was his turn to ask a question.

"So? What did you think?"

"I have to admit," she said, sitting back. "That was the best steak I've ever had. It was cooked to perfection."

"And the pie?"

"The same," she said.

"So you'll write about this place in your newspaper?"

"Definitely."

"Can we tell him now?"

"Why not?" she asked. "There's no name outside. If I'm going to tell people to come here, I'm going to need to know the name of the place."

When Hank came back, Butler introduced M.J. as the editor of the *Dodge City Times*.

"She wants to write about your place."

"Write about it?" Hank frowned.

"Tell people to come here and eat," Butler said. "Once she's done you won't have an empty seat in the house, ever."

Curiously, Hank did not look as happy about this as Butler had thought he would.

"I don't know, Mr. Butler ..." he said.

"What's the problem?"

Hank looked at M.J.

"I really appreciate the offer, Miss," he said, "but I'm all alone here. I don't think I'd be able to handle it if it was crowded all the time. I kinda like it the way it is."

"But... you're not making a living here, are you, Hank?" Butler asked. "I thought you wanted people to come?"

"Well, sure ... every once in a while." He looked directly at M.J. again. "I don't mean to be ungrateful ..."

"Hey, don't worry," she said. "If you don't want me to write about it, I won't write about it."

"Is it okay if I think about it some?" he asked finally.

"Of course," she said. "Just let Butler know what you want to do, and he'll tell me."

"Okay," he said. "Thanks." He went back to the kitchen.

"That's odd," Butler said.

"Curious," she said, "but it could be that he's happy the way things are."

"That wasn't the impression I first got when I spoke with him," Butler said.

"Hey," she said, "not everybody wants the world to know where they are every minute, you know?"

Actually, he did know that, better than most.

* * *

They paid the bill and left. Butler walked her back home and along the way she kept asking questions. As they neared her house she got to the one he didn't want to answer.

"So, what brought you to the West?"

Suddenly, as he pondered how to answer the question, he realized how Hank must have felt.

"Much like every other young man," he lied, "I came to see what it was like."

"And you planned all along to gamble your way across?" she asked.

"Pretty much," he said. "There's not much else I can do."

"You seem pretty intelligent," she commented. "Seems to me you could do anything you put your mind to. I'll even bet you're college educated."

They stopped right in front of her house.

"Well," he said, "this was nice."

She smiled at him, examined his face.

"Don't want to answer those last few, huh?"

"Too personal," he said. "I'm not ready to put my person life on display in a newspaper."

"I see."

"You see," he said, "but do you understand?"

She thought a moment, then said, "I suppose so. I mean, as the newspaperwoman—the daughter of a newspaperman—I tend to think everything should be in the newspaper, but then I realize not everyone thinks that way."

"Your father started the *Times*?" he asked.

"Yes," she said. "He came here in 1871, along with the others."

"The others?"

"He came with Chalk Beeson and Dog Kelley and the other Dodge City fathers."

"So he was part of the Dodge City Gang?"

"Not part of the Gang, not part of the Reformers. Well, there were hardly any Reformers back then, but my father tried to straddle the fence as much as he could while reporting the news."

"And what happened to him?"

"Dodge City was a wild town, even just a few years ago. About five years ago he was in the wrong place at the wrong time and he caught a bullet. Since then my brother and I have tried to keep the paper going."

"Younger brother?"

"Yes," she said. "It's hard trying to run the paper and him at the same time, but ... he's my brother."

"He's old enough," Butler said, "to run his own life."

"If you knew him better you wouldn't say that," she said. "Well, I better get inside. I'm an early-to-bed kind of person. Thank you for the supper, and the interview."

"It was my pleasure."

As they shook hands she said, "Yeah, but you didn't think it was going to be, did you?"

He watched her walk up the three steps, almost trip on the second loose one, and go inside before he turned and walked away.

Instead of heading for a saloon or back to his hotel Butler found himself going back to Hank's place. When he entered he found the man sitting at one of his own tables, waiting for him.

"I thought you'd be back."

"Curiosity, is all," Butler said.

"I appeciate you tryin' to help me," Hank said. "Yer probably wondering why I reacted the way I did."

"You know, I was wondering," Butler said, "but then halfway I realized you don't owe me any explanation."

"That's true," Hank said, "but I think I'd like to give you one." He stood up. "Come into the kitchen with me."

He led Butler into the kitchen, which was so cramped there was barely room for the two of them and the stove. In one corner, however, was a wooden chest. Hank stopped and pressed his knee against it, turning to face Butler.

"I don't know," he said, "but I have a feeling about you. I have a feeling you'll understand."

"Understand what?"

"My past is in this chest."

"Your past ... as a blacksmith?"

"That's only part of it," Hank said. "See, I think we all live our lives in sections. I'm almost fifty now, maybe in the last part of my life, maybe not. But the part of my life that I don't want anyone to know about is in this chest."

Hank leaned over, his back to Butler, opened the chest and reached inside. When he straightened and turned he was holding a gun, and Butler's stomach clenched. But then he saw that the gun was holstered, and the belt was wrapped around. Hank turned and showed the holstered weapon to Butler.

"Now do you understand?"

"Yeah," Butler said, "I think I do."

CHAPTER 26

Red Sandland, Willy, and Dave came out of the Red Dog Saloon, staggering. They'd stayed longer than they'd intended, and they were all close to falling down drunk.

"I say we just find 'im and kill 'im," Dave slurred.

"Find 'im and kill 'im?" Willy asked. "You can't even stand up straight."

"Shut up, both of you," Sandland said. "We ain't in no shape to kill anybody, 'cept maybe ourselves. We best stay out of this gambler's way tonight."

"So where we goin'?" Willy asked.

"Where else?" Sandland asked. "Back to the district."

"Oh, yeah," Dave said, "we can't possibly get killed there ..."

Hank locked the front door and they sat and talked over a pot of coffee.

"Not that anyone will try to come in," he said after locking it.

"I don't understand," Butler said, when they were seated. "If you don't want people around you, why would you open a restaurant—and in Dodge City, of all places?"

"Dodge ain't what it used to be," Hank said. "People are leavin' here. I thought it was better to start here than someplace like Tombstone, which is growing, or Denver, which has just too damn many people."

"Is your face that recognizable?" Butler, himself, had left home ten years before, but had only been in the West for six or seven, and did not know all of the "legends" on sight.

"No," Hank said, "I don't think so. My name, though, if anyone heard it, would ring a bell."

"Hank?"

"No," Hank said, "that's not my real name."

"You know what?" Butler said. "I don't need to know your real name. I don't need to know the man who's in that trunk in the kitchen. You're the man I've met, and it's only you I have to know."

Hank smiled and extended his hand.

"Henry Pryor, at your service."

Butler took his hand, shook it and said, "Happy to meet you."

Butler didn't leave then. Hank produced a bottle of whiskey, which they used to lace their coffee. Butler did not want to end up drunk. He still had a full night of poker ahead of him.

They did not discuss their pasts, only their present and a little bit of their futures. Hank lived upstairs, so when Butler was ready to leave Hank unlocked the door and let him out.

"I hope I confided in the right person," he said, "and this story won't end up all over town."

"The only story that's going to get spread all over town is one you tell yourself, Hank," Butler said. "This is all just between you and me."

"Thanks, Butler."

As they shook hands Butler asked, "Do you want me to tell M.J. that you're not interested in being written about?"

"No, that's okay," Hank said. "I'll talk to her and tell her myself."

"Good night, then."

Hank closed and locked the door behind Butler and blew out the lamps. Butler headed back to Front Street.

Butler decided to try the Long Branch for his poker tonight. Maybe later he'd check out the Alhambra and see if Ben Thompson was there. As soon as he entered the Long Branch, though, he saw that it wouldn't be necessary. Ben Thompson was seated at a table in the center of the room with five other men, deeply engrossed in playing five-card stud.

"It's a stud table," Bill Harris said, coming up next to Butler. "No other games."

"I see."

"Interested? I could probably start another table."

"I think I'll have a beer first," Butler said, "but thanks."

He didn't like having Bill Harris come right up to him when he entered. If the man continued to do it, he'd mark the Long Branch off his list and do his gambling elsewhere.

He bellied up to the bar and ordered a beer, then turned with it in hand to observe the place for a while.

Butler never rushed into a game. He preferred to watch and assess both the venue, and the table. From his vantage point he was able to watch Thompson and his opponents as they did battle. Off to the right was a second table, which seemed to be dealer's choice. He watched that one, as well. Around him there was also a faro game going, a roulette wheel, a red dog table and couple of tables featuring blackjack, a game he hated.

He was content for the moment to sip his beer and watch.

During the next hour two girls approached him. They were pretty but he wasn't interested in a girl, at the moment. He suspected that Bill Harris had sent them.

He finished his beer and set the empty mug down on the bar. He was not tempted to have a second. He was feeling the effects of the first one, combined with the whiskey he'd drunk with Hank. He decided to take a walk around the room before deciding which table to sit in on.

He wondered as he made a circuit of the room if any of the men in that place knew who he was, and were laying for him? He had not seen the man from the hotel hallway anywhere, but that didn't mean he didn't have some friends representing him. Probably the smartest thing for him to do was leave Dodge City in the morning, but wherever he went they'd probably track him. Better to face them in Dodge and get it over with. Maybe after back-to-back tries—Wichita and Dodge—he'd have a breather. During his walk around the room,

Butler momentarily gave in to curiosity and speculated about Hank Pryor, and what his real identity might be; but he immediately set it aside. After all, he preferred not to talk about his own past, although he was not running away from a misspent part of his life, as Hank might have been.

Butler watched a bit of roulette and red dog, and just enough of blackjack to know that he had not changed his mind about the game. He found the faro layout interesting and wondered who the dealer was, but wasn't curious enough to ask on the spot. And so he ended up back by the two poker tables. At the stud table Ben Thompson was still holding court. He noticed Butler watching and inclined his head in a slight nod of welcome. The table was using chips, and Thompson had twice as much in front of him as anyone else. He was having a good night, and it was better to avoid a gambler who was riding a wave of good luck.

At the other table, where the game was dealer's choice, the chips seemed equally divided among four players as a fifth man busted out of the game and left. Butler moved quickly to take the vacated spot. The stakes were not very high at this point, so he bought two hundred dollars worth of chips and settled in to see how the night's luck was going to run.

CHAPTER 27

As it turned out his luck was running fair, and he easily outclassed all the other players at the table. At one point during the evening he noticed Ben Thompson looking his way. The man nodded slightly toward the bar, which Butler took to mean he wanted to meet there. Both men excused themselves from the table with a muttered, "Deal me out a couple of hands," and went to the bar. By the time Butler arrived Thompson had two beers waiting.

"How are you doin' tonight?" Thompson asked.

"I'm doing well," Butler said. "The cards are running hot and cold, but I don't have much competition at the table."

"Same here," Thompson said. "You want to sit at the same table?"

"I see the mountain of chips you got in front of you, Ben," Butler said. "I think your cards are running a little better than you say. Why do I get the feeling you're just trying to lure me over to your table?"

Thompson laughed. "I'm just looking for some

competition, is all. Makes the game a little more interesting."

"I don't mind an interesting game," Butler said, "but
I'm also trying to make a living here. Going against you
while your luck is running isn't exactly the way to do
that."

"You're too smart for your own good," Thompson
said. "Anyway, it's nice just to have you in the room,
watching my back. And don't worry, I'm watching
yours, too."

"Speaking of that ..." Butler said, and he went on to
tell Thompson about the curious man in the hall.

"Does this happen to you a lot?" the other man
asked.

"Yes."

Thompson put up a hand. "I won't ask why. Just be
assured I'll be watching for a man matching that de-
scription. Apparently, at the moment, we're the only
two decent poker players in town. We've got to watch
out for each other."

"I heard Luke Short might be on his way here," Butler
offered.

"Well, that would be interesting."

"Have you played with him before?"

"Luke and I have sat across from each other many
times. In fact, I've pretty much played with every decent
poker player in the West—now that I've played with
you, I mean."

"Ever play with a fellow named Three-Fingered
Jack?"

"Well, since you said last night that you came here
from Wichita, I suspect you mean Three-Eyed Jack.

Hell, I thought Jack was dead. Is he still in Wichita?"

"Still there."

"Did I pass the test?"

"Well ..." Butler said, and let it drop.

"I've got to get back to my table," Thompson said. "The beer is on me. If you feel like some stud later, just move on over."

"I'll do it, Ben."

Thompson touched his hat and made his way back to his table, where he managed to sit down without knocking over the mountain of chips in front of him.

Butler went back to his own table and started building a mountain of his own.

Butler's game broke up only after several hours, after he managed to take chips from everyone who sat in on the game. Given the option of moving to Ben Thompson's stud game or to one of the other saloons in town, he opted for the shorter trip.

"About time," Thompson said, when he sat down. "I've been waiting for some competition."

Since he had built himself a nice stake from the other table, Butler decided to just sit back and enjoy the rest of the evening. He caught three aces in his first hand, which elicited groans from the other players who, up to now, only had Ben Thompson's luck to contend with.

"Boys," Thompson said, as Butler raked in the pot, "the price of poker has just gone up."

For the next hour, chips went either to Butler or to Ben Thompson, at an even pace. Only the other players at the table were suffering losses, and, one by one, they busted out of the game. There were others watching, but they did not attempt to fill the empty seats. Off to one side Bill Harris watched with a big smile on his face. Having two quality poker players in the house was good for business. Even if the other patrons were just watching the action, they were drinking while they did it.

Finally, about two in the morning, Ben Thompson and Tyrone Butler were playing head to head. Each pot was in the hundreds, sometimes thousands of dollars, but two evenly matched players competing head to head usually meant an even exchange of chips over a period of time. By three A.M. both men agreed to call a halt to the game.

"Unless ..." Thompson said.

"Unless what?" Butler asked.

"You want to play one last hand, winner take all?"

"All?"

"Just what we have on the table," Thompson said. "Not our wallets."

Butler was willing. After all, he had bought in for two hundred when they started, and had been playing on that ever since. Now he had nearly five thousand dollars in front of him, and figured Ben Thompson for about the same.

"All right," Butler said, and word spread quickly through the saloon that a winnertake-all hand was about to take place between Ben Thompson and the new gambler in town, Butler.

"We're putting on a show for the sports," Thompson said.

"I think we need an impartial dealer," Butler said.

"I agree."

Thompson looked around, located Bill Harris, and waved him over to the table.

"Bill, you got a lovely young lady here who can deal?"

"I got just the gal for you, Ben," Harris said. He called one of the girls over. She came running up excitedly, thinking she was going to get to deal, but Harris said to her, "Go and get Trixie."

As it turned out Trixie was the faro dealer Butler had been watching earlier in the night. She was tall, with long red hair and a creamy swell of freckled bosom rising out of her emerald green dress.

"Trixie, these gents would like you to deal one hand for them, winner take all."

Trixie looked at the chips on the table and said, "That's got to be ten thousand dollars, Bill."

"Almost to the penny," Butler said, impressed.

"Will you do it?" Harris asked her.

She smiled and said, "I'd be honored."

CHAPTER 28

⊷●⊶

Trixie took her seat among a rustling of silk, gathered up the cards, and said to Harris, "May I have a new deck?"

Harris went to the bar and got a new deck from the bartender. Trixie opened it and expertly shuffled the cards while both Butler and Ben Thompson watched in admiration.

"All right, gents," she said, "here we go."

She dealt them each a card down and a card up. Butler got a king, while Thompson received an ace.

"Mr. Thompson's bet," she said, then corrected herself. "Oh, sorry, this is winner take all, right?"

"That's correct," Thompson said.

"Then I beg your pardon," she said. "Next card."

She dealt Thompson a deuce and Butler a three.

"Not much help there," she announced. "Next card."

Thompson got a five.

An eight to Butler.

"Not much developing here," Trixie said. "Last card."

Thompson got an ace, pairing him on the table. Butler got a pair also, receiving another eight.

"Pair of aces to a pair of eights," Trixie said.

"Well, if we were betting, I guess I'd be betting my lungs," Thompson said.

"And I'd be calling."

"Would you, now?"

"Definitely."

Thompson stared at Butler's cards.

"How would you like to up the bet?"

Now it was Butler's turn to stare at the cards on the table and think.

"You know what, Ben?" he said, finally. "I'm not going to do that. I'm just going to go with what we have on the table."

"Showdown, Gents," Trixie said.

Thompson turned over his hole card. A second deuce.

"Aces over deuces," Trixie said, "two pair for Mr. Thompson. That's a damn good hand in stud, especially two-handed."

Butler turned over his hole card. It was an eight, giving him three of them.

"But that's a better hand," Trixie said. "Three eights to Mr. Butler, the winner."

Thompson smiled, spread his hands, then reached across the table to shake hands with Butler. They both then took one of Trixie's hands and kissed it.

"Why, gentlemen," she said, in a fake southern accent, "ya'll are gonna give me the vapors."

Bill Harris stepped in and asked, "How would the three of you like a drink on the house?"

"You got any brandy behind that bar, Bill?" Thompson asked.

"I believe I could scrounge up a bottle, Ben."

Thompson looked at Butler, who said, "Why not? Trixie?"

"I'm game," she said. "I usually drink whiskey, but brandy'll do if it's free."

Bill Harris brought over a bottle of brandy and four glasses as things got back to normal around them. He sat down with them and poured out four glasses.

"You mind if I join you?" he asked.

"Not at all, Bill," Thompson said.

"I was watching you deal faro earlier," Butler said to Trixie. "You're very good."

"Not that good," she said. "Most of the men who play at my table are too busy looking down my dress."

"Hey," Thompson said to her, "you use what you've got, right? If you win, you're good."

"Well, thank you, both," she said. "Maybe you should tell that to my boss." She finished her brandy and stood up. "Gentlemen, time for this lady to turn in. Good night."

They all stood as she walked away, watching until she was up the stairs and gone.

"You got a good one there, Bill," Thompson said.

"I know it." He picked up the brandy bottle. "See you gents here tomorrow night?"

"Maybe," Butler said.

"Maybe not," Thompson said. "I just took a big hit here. Might try my luck someplace else."

"Well," Harris said, "I hope it's here." He looked at Butler. "Let me know when you want to cash those in."

As he walked away Butler said, "You're luck was running good all night, until that last hand."

"It only takes one," Thompson told him. "What about your luck? Three running eights?"

"Like you say," Butler answered, "it only takes one."

"Or," Ben Thompson added with a loud laugh, "in this case three, huh?"

Butler cashed in his chips with Bill Harris while Thompson had a beer at the bar.

"You're makin' a name for yourself in Dodge," Harris said.

"It wasn't my intention," Butler said. "There's enough men who've made names for themselves here. I'm not looking to join that group."

"Don't know if you have much choice now," Harris said. "What if Chalk and I make it worth your while?"

"How do you mean?"

"Make it worth your while to gamble here, exclusively."

"For how long?"

Harris shrugged. "We can come to some agreement."

Butler accepted his cash from Harris and said, "Let me think about it."

"All right," Harris said. "That's all I ask."

Butler met Ben Thompson at the bar and told him about Bill Harris's offer.

"Ah, you don't want to do that," Thompson said.

"Why not?"

"Why limit your options?" the other man asked.

"You've got suckers in every saloon in town. Why give that up?"

Butler listened and nodded.

"You never intended to take him up on it, did you?" Thompson asked.

"What makes you say that?"

"You're too smart."

"I'm not going to be here long enough to make that kind of deal worthwhile."

"Whatever the reason," Thompson said. "I've got to get these old bones to bed."

Butler doubted Thompson was a year or two older than he was, but he knew what the man meant. His own bones were feeling kind of old.

"Me too."

"Dodge House?" Thompson asked.

"That's right."

"Me too. Best hotel in town. Let's walk over together."

"You sure you want to do that?"

"Look," Thompson said, "for whatever reason you're a target, there's just as many reasons why I'm one. You could get hit by lead meant for me just as easily as I could get hit by lead meant for you. At least this way we're able to watch each other's back."

"Okay," Butler said. "Let's do it."

"Besides," Thompson added, "you're carrying a lot of my cash, and I don't want anybody trying to take it from you before I get a chance to."

"Your concern is touching."

CHAPTER 29

Updegraff found Red Sandland and his two partners in a popular Front Street café the next morning, having breakfast.

"What happened?" he asked, sitting down. He spoke to Sandland, ignored the other two. All three men seemed to be suffering after the night before.

"Couldn't get it done yesterday, Al," Sandland said, "but don't worry. It'll get done."

"I know you couldn't get it done yesterday," Updegraff said. "That's obvious. What I want to know is why?"

"He spotted me," Sandland said. "He got suspicious. That meant we couldn't catch him by surprise."

"So now he knows you three are after him?"

"He only saw me," Sandland said, "he didn't see Dave and Willy."

Updegraff stared at the other two men, who were concentrating on their flapjacks. To him "Dave and Willy" sounded like a circus act. Maybe he'd picked the wrong men for this job, but he'd already paid them most of the money Peacock had given him.

"All right," he said. "Get it done today or tomorrow, and don't spend the money until you do."

"You sayin' you're gonna want the money back?"

"If you don't do the job."

Sandland studied Updegraff for a few moments. He knew the man had been a lawman in his time, albeit a crooked one. He also knew that his brother-in-law, A. J. Peacock, was a fair hand with a gun. So he figured, better to do the job than *not* do it and try to keep the money—some of which had already been spent on whores and whiskey.

"Like I said," he replied, "don't worry. The job'll get done."

"Okay," Updegraff said, standing up. "I'll let Anthony know we got nothin' to worry about."

It took Sandland a moment to realize that Updegraff was talking about Peacock.

After Updegraff had left Sandland got the attention of Dave and Willy by slamming his hand down on the table.

"Wha—" Dave asked. Willy looked around, his eyes wild.

"Tonight we stay sober and do the job."

"I'm in favor of stayin' sober," Willy said. "I feel like crap."

"Sure didn't effect your appetite," Dave said.

"Nothin' effects his appetite," Sandland said.

He turned his attention to his own breakfast. He didn't have to wonder what Peacock and Updegraff had against this gambler, Butler. He'd heard how the man had backed Jim Masterson's play in the Lady Gay. It was well known in Dodge that Masterson and Peacock were on the outs. Without the gambler around, Masterson would be an easier target, even with Neal Brown backing him.

Sandland just wondered what Peacock and Updegraff were going to do about Bat Masterson after they killed his brother Jim. Well, that wouldn't be any concern of his. He didn't mind bushwhacking a gambler, but they'd have to pay him a lot more money to go up against Bat Masterson.

A lot more!

Butler had breakfast in the hotel. It was just more convenient that way. As he entered he didn't see Dog Kelley anywhere. Either the ex-mayor had eaten and gone, or he'd decided to change up his routine today.

He did, however, see Ben Thompson at a table. As if he sensed he was being watch, Ben looked up, smiled and waved Butler to join him. Butler thought they were either going to end up very good friends, or sick of each other.

"'Morning," Thompson greeted. "If you're not sick of me yet have a seat and join me."

"Seems to me you'd be the one feeling that way," Butler said.

"What, you mean after last night?" Thompson asked. "That was fun, son."

"Losing is fun?"

"Well," the other man said, "not as much fun as winning, but you can't take this stuff too seriously."

"I suppose not."

Thompson had not yet ordered so the waiter came over and took orders from them both—steak and eggs for Thompson, bacon and eggs for Butler.

"Any sign of your man today?" Thompson asked.

"No," Butler said, "and so far I don't seem to be drawing any obvious attention."

"Enjoy it, then," Thompson said, "with the Earps gone, Bat Masterson and Bill Tilghman and Luke Short and the like, this town is looking for new blood."

"Like you?"

"Me? I'm old blood," Thompson said. "You're the one who's new blood."

"I like my blood just the way it is, thanks."

"Then let me warn you about the editor of the town newspaper. She's got charm and looks, and, if you're not careful, she'll talk you into an interview."

Butler looked away.

"Ah, I see I'm too late."

"Did it last night, at supper.,"

"Ah," Thompson said. "You got her to eat with you. Good man. We did mine in the hotel lobby. When is it going to run?"

"I don't know," Butler said. "She didn't confide that."

"Probably in the next couple of days," Thompson said. "You want my advice, make your money and get out. If you weren't a target before, you will be after that."

Butler thought Thompson was kidding, but couldn't tell by looking at him.

CHAPTER 30

Kevin Ryerson rode into Dodge while Butler and Ben Thompson were having breakfast. The day's business had already started and Front Street had enough going on that no one paid him any special mind. He wore nondescript trail clothes, and rode an equally unremarkable-looking mare. There was nothing about the man that would make anyone notice him, which was the way he preferred it.

He found the livery, put up his horse, and then asked the liveryman for a cheap hotel. He wasn't looking for something cheap so much as something out of the way. Armed with directions, he walked back through town carrying his saddlebags and rifle. He'd never been to Dodge City before, and was not particularly impressed with its history. He took Dodge's reputation the same way he took the reputation of men—with a grain of salt. Too many times he had found the reputations of men to be overblown and unearned. Why should a town be any different?

He passed the Dodge House and gave it a brief look. He knew the kind of people who'd be staying there. Swells, gamblers, high-class ladies—none of them his kind of people.

He found his hotel, a somewhat rundown establishment that, nevertheless, was this side of the red-light district. He checked in, got a room overlooking the street, dumped his belonging on the bed. The mattress was thin, but it was better than sitting on the ground. He had a steak on his mind, and a drink, and then after that he'd get down to business.

Butler and Thompson finished breakfast and left the Dodge House together.

"I'm off to the local gunsmith," Thompson said. "I need some work done on my Peacemaker." He indicated the single-action Colt Peacemaker on his hip.

It was the days that were difficult for a gambler, finding something to do while they waited for the saloons and gambling halls to open.

"I believe I'll try to find myself an afternoon poker game," Butler said. He'd waited most of yesterday, ended up playing only at night and did quite well. If his luck was good, he might as well press it during the day, he thought.

"Good luck to you, then," Thompson said. "Maybe we'll find ourselves at the same table again tonight."

The two bade one another good day and went their separate ways.

Red Sandland watched as Butler and Ben Thompson went in opposite directions. That suited him. He did not want to be anywhere near Ben Thompson when the man had a gun in his hand.

Sandland had actually done something smart, which qualified this a landmark day in his life. He had positioned both Willy and Dave so that when Butler left his hotel, none of the three of them had to tail him. They were stationed in such a way that they could monitor his progress all along Front Street. If he happened to leave Front Street they'd be in big trouble, but lucky for them he didn't. He went directly to the Lady Gay and tried the front door, which happened to be open even though the saloon was not.

As he went in, the three men left their positions to meet up directly across the street from the saloon.

When Butler walked into the Lady Gay, Al Updegraff was using a broom on the floor in front of the bar. He looked up, saw Butler, and froze. His gun was behind the bar. If Sandland and his idiots had named Updegraff as the man who sent them to try and kill him, he was in trouble.

As it happened, Butler smiled at him and asked, "Is Jim Masterson around?"

"We're closed," Updegraff said. "I just got the door open to get some air."

"I can see that," Butler said. "I'm looking for Masterson."

Updegraff jerked his chin upward and said, "He ain't come down yet."

"I think I'll wait for him."

"Suit yourself." Updegraff had considered kicking Butler out, but decided against it.

"You the bartender?"

"That's me," Updegraff said. "Bartender, and swamper."

"Let me ask you. What do you think the chances are of me getting up an afternoon poker game?"

Updegraff stopped sweeping and leaned on the broom handle, holding it in both hands.

"Pretty damned good, I'd say," he answered. "The town's full of gamblers. Not good ones, but gamblers."

"That's what I heard."

"Seems I saw you in here before," Updegraff said, pretending not to recognize Butler.

"That's because I've been in here before."

"Last night," the barkeep said, "you were playing poker with Ben Thompson."

"So I was."

Updegraff used his broom to get himself close to the door. He peered out the window and saw Sandland across the street with Dave and Willy. This was good. They had Butler spotted. Updegraff decided to do what he could to keep Butler there, until the three men decided their plan.

"Got some coffee on," he told Butler. "Wanna cup?"

"Sure," Butler said, "thanks."

"I just got to go back to the kitchen," Updegraff said. "I'll be right back."

Butler nodded, watched the man go behind the bar and disappear through a doorway, broom and all.

"What do we do?" Willy asked.

"The Lady Gay is closed," Dave said. "We gotta wait."

"We don't gotta wait," Sandland said. "The front door's open, there ain't nobody in there but Al Updegraff."

"How do you know that?" Willy asked.

"I seen him sweepin'."

"So what do we do?" Willy asked.

"We go in," Sandland said. "We go in and we take him."

"Now?" Dave asked.

"Right now," Sandland said. "Check your guns. We don't want no mistakes."

As they checked their loads they didn't notice the man watching them. He had come down the street, spotted them, and stopped to watch. Now, as they were checking their weapons, he knew just what they had in mind.

From the kitchen Updegraff looked outside to see what Sandland and the others were doing. When he saw them all draw their guns and check them, he knew they were ready. He poured a cup of coffee and went back into the saloon.

Butler watched the bartender walk toward him with a cup of steaming coffee.

"There ya go," Updegraff said, setting it in front of him.

"Much obliged."

As Updegraff wiped his hands on the apron he was wearing, he saw the batwing doors swing inward quietly. Red Sandland appeared, gun in hand. Behind him came his two partners. Updegraff had to get out of the line of fire, and fast.

"I gotta get back to work," he said to Butler, and scurried to get to the safety of the bar.

At that moment Butler saw the three men who had entered, recognized the one in the center. They were fanned out in front of the door, facing him. If not for the bartender, he might have noticed them sooner. The bartender had suddenly ducked down behind the bar ...

"I was wondering when I'd see you again," Butler said. "Brought some friends, I see."

"Mister," Sandland said, "we ain't here to talk."

"Well, if you're here to bushwhack me you're out of luck. I never sit with my back to the door. It's a bad habit. You should've come in a window, or a back door."

"It don't matter," the middle man, Sandland, said. "We got you three to one."

"Fair odds, do you think?"

"Mister," Red Sandland said, "fair ain't got nothin' to do with nothin'."

"You're right about that," Butler said. He picked up the cup of coffee with his left hand and sipped it. He could see that the nonchalant move unnerved the men.

Undoubtedly, they were wondering why he wasn't more worried, or scared.

It wouldn't do to have them know he was both.

CHAPTER 31

Butler didn't waste any more time. He put the coffee cup down, slid his hand beneath the table and then upended it. He came to his feet, drew his gun, and fired. It didn't matter who fired the first shot. The three men were there to kill him, of that he had no doubt. Giving them the first shot would have just been foolish.

Sandland, seeing the table start to tip over, hurriedly drew his gun and shouted, "Get him!"

Their initial volley of shots struck the table, gouging out chunks of it. Butler's first shot was a hurried one, as much to scatter the men as hit one. It worked on both counts. The bullet nicked Willy's arm as the three men dove for cover. Dave took cover at the far end of the bar while both Willy and Sandland found their own tables to overturn.

Butler fired two more times, blindly, from behind his table, and then suddenly the saloon grew quiet. The sound of empty shells hitting the floor filed the room as all the parties reloaded. Butler knew if they charged him they could kill him, but he'd get at least one, and he was betting that none of the three of them wanted to be that one.

"Come on, boys," he invited. "Charge me all at once. Let's see what happens."

Outside on the street, people heard the shots from inside the Lady Gay, but only one man moved toward the saloon. As he crossed the street Kevin Ryerson was drawing his gun. While other folks backed away or ran for cover, they couldn't help but wonder who this man was heading toward the trouble, and not away from it.

Jim Masterson heard the initial shots and fell out of bed in his haste to reach for his gun. When he heard the shots continue he realized nobody was shooting at him. It took a moment for him to wake up enough to realize it was coming from downstairs. Hastily, he reached for his pants ...

Butler fired more blind shots and then suddenly a fourth man was coming through the front door. He wasted no time in joining the fray. He turned and shot Dave, who was hiding at the end of the bar. The bullet took him in the neck, and then a second took his life.

Butler stood just as both Willy and Red Sandland did the same. Sandland saw him, tried to bring his gun to bear, but Butler shot him in the chest. Both Butler and Ryerson pointed their guns as Willy but it was Jim Masterson who shot him from the second floor, one clean shot right through the heart.

Butler first looked up at Masterson, who was leaning on the railing, then over at Ryerson, who he didn't know.

"What the hell—" Masterson said, from upstairs.

"You might as well take the time to get dressed," Butler called to him. "I don't think there are any more."

"I'll be right down." He turned and went back into his room.

Now Butler looked at Ryerson and said, "I'm much obliged, Mister . . ."

"Ryerson," the man said, "Kevin Ryerson. I was just passin' by, thought I might could help."

"You thought right."

"What did these three jaspers have against you?"

"Can't say I know," Butler replied. "I don't know any of the three of them."

Ryerson ejected the spent shells from his gun, reloaded and holstered it. Butler could see the callus on the thumb of his right hand. He was a man who used his gun a lot, probably even practiced with it.

Butler did the same, made sure his gun was fully loaded before he holstered his as well.

"Well, I think I owe you a drink, Mr. Ryerson, but we better get it before the law arrives."

"Suits me."

"Bartender!"

Al Updegraff peered up over the bar, saw that Butler was still alive and inwardly cursed.

"Yes, sir?"

"Whiskey for me and my friend."

"We're, uh, closed, Mister."

"Well, open up," Butler said. "We deserve a drink."

"I can't just open—"

"Do it, Al," Jim Masterson said, coming down the stairs, "and pour me one, too."

Updegraff looked at Masterson, then shrugged and said, "It's your whiskey."

"You're damn right it is."

Masterson reached the bar at the same time Butler and Ryerson did. Updegraff poured three whiskeys and they all picked them up.

"Jim Masterson," Butler said, "meet Kevin Ryerson."

"Pleased to meet you," Jim said.

"Same here," Ryerson commented.

The three men clinked glasses and downed their drinks. For Jim Masterson it was a harsh breakfast.

Fire burning in his stomach, Masterson said, "Now does somebody want to tell me what the hell is goin' on here?"

CHAPTER 32

By the time City Marshal Fred Singer arrived, Masterson and Butler had moved the bodies to one part of the saloon. Masterson had also instructed Updegraff to get some help and bring in some new tables before it was time to open. To his surprise, Updegraff complied with his wishes. He figured the man just wanted to get out of there before more lead started flying.

When Singer arrived Butler and Ryerson were in front of the bar, and Masterson was behind it.

"What's goin' on, Jim?" he asked. "The Lady Gay startin' to specialize in collectin' bodies?"

"You tell me, Fred," Masterson said. "These three men busted in here and tried to kill Butler."

"Mr. Butler," Singer said, "you again."

"Not again, Marshal," Butler corrected. "Last time I was just helping Jim, here. This time it was the other way around."

"And who are you, sir?" Singer asked Ryerson.

"Just somebody who was passin' by and stopped to help."

"Passin' by, or passin' through?" Singer asked.

"Well, I rode through the night to get here this mornin'," Ryerson said. "Figured to have some breakfast and get some sleep."

"But you got yourself involved in a shooting."

"Well," Ryerson said, "like I said, I was passin' by. If there's no more trouble, I'd just as soon go and get some steak and eggs before I turn in."

"And when you wake up?" Singer asked. "Will you be leavin' us then?"

"Marshal," Ryerson said, "I guess I'll make that decision when I wake up. Gents."

Butler and Masterson both nodded to Ryerson, who took his leave of the situation.

"He was just bein' helpful, Fred," Masterson said. "Don't be so hard on him."

"Don't tell me how to do my job, Jim," Singer said. "You're not wearin' a badge anymore."

"No, you're right," Masterson said, "I'm not, you are. In fact, you're wearin' my badge, Fred."

Singer firmed his jaw and said, "It's mine now, Jim."

"Well then, earn it," Masterson said, harshly. "Get these bodies out of my place, and how about findin' out who they were and why they wanted Butler dead?"

Singer got right up in Jim Masterson's face. But Butler could see the man was not completely confident.

"I'll do my job, Jim," he said tightly. "Maybe if you'd paid more attention to doin' yours and forgot about being a saloon owner you'd still be wearin' a badge." Singer turned and walked to the front door, then turned to face them again. "I'll be back with some men to clean up this mess. Mr Butler?"

"Yeah?'

"You shoot one more person and I'm gonna have to ask you to leave Dodge."

"Sheriff," Butler said, "I'll consider myself warned."

After Singer left Butler was alone in the saloon with Jim Masterson, who poured two more drinks.

"I ain't had this much whiskey for breakfast in years," he said, after he'd downed it. "You wanna tell me what's goin' on?"

"Not sure I know," Butler said.

"Who were those three?"

"Friends of those fellas who tried for you the other night?" Butler asked. "Maybe they're mad at me for helping you?"

"Uh-huh," Masterson said. "What else you got?"

"Friends of that fella I busted out of the poker game the other night? Got wrote up in the papers. Maybe he's mad."

"His father would have his balls if he pulled a stunt like this," Masterson said. "Keep goin'."

"You got something you want to say?" Butler asked.

"I'm thinkin' maybe you carry some trouble around with you," the ex-lawman said.

"Doesn't everybody?"

"I'm thinkin' the deadly kind, with you," Masterson said. "You ain't wanted anyplace, are you? Carryin' a price on your head?"

It was a trick question, and he answered it the only way he thought he could.

"Not by the law."

They stared at each other for a few moments and then

before Jim Masterson could ask another question, the
batwing doors admitted two more people.

"Look who I found out front." Neal Brown said. Entering with him was M.J. Healy, pad in hand.

"Well, what happened here?" she asked, looking
around. Her eyes came to light on the three bodies. Un-
affected, she walked over to them and bent over to take
a look.

"That's Red Sandland," she said.

"Which one?" Masterson asked.

"The one with the red hair," she said dryly, straighten-
ing up.

"You know the other two?"

"Cronies of his," she said. "I don't know their
names."

"How do you know his?" Brown asked.

"It's my job to know people and things in this town,"
she said, "and I do my job well."

She got no argument from any of the men.

"So tell us about him," Masterson asked. "Who was
Red Sandland?"

"Fella who thought he was a hard man," she said. "I
guess he was wrong."

"For hire?"

"Yep," she said, "and it wouldn't take much, either.
Whatever somebody offered him, it'd be more than he
had."

"Neal, you see anybody else loitering about out
front?" Masterson asked.

Brown went to one of the front windows and looked
out.

"Nobody suspicious," he said. "Folks are still starin' over here, but that's only natural."

"Butler, why don't you tell M.J. what happened here?" Masterson suggested.

"Why?" Butler asked.

"Let her write about it," Masterson said. "Let folks know what can happen if they get out of line in the Lady Gay."

"Two nights this week," M.J. said. "That's lettin' them know, all right."

Butler saw Masterson's point, though. Whoever those men were, whether they were there for him because of something that had happened in Dodge, or because of a price that was still on his head from back East, they ought to send out a message that said, "You got to come with more than that."

"Well," he said, "I came over here looking for an early poker game …"

CHAPTER 33

Marshal Fred Singer returned with several men and the bodies were carried out and over to the undertaker. Masterson, Neal Brown, and Butler did not offer to help. By the time they arrived Butler had told the whole story to M.J. So when Singer left she left with him, to interview him about how his time on the job was going, so far.

"Well," Butler heard him say as he and M.J. left, "if it wasn't for that new gambler, Butler, it'd be a damn sight easier ..."

After they'd gone Butler looked around and noticed that Al Updegraff had not returned.

"Your bartender," he said to Masterson.

"What about him?"

"He knew something."

"What makes you say that?"

"First he was trying to get rid of me," Butler said, "and then suddenly he offered me a cup of coffee. Also, he took cover behind the bar pretty damn quick."

"Well, that doesn't surprise me," Masterson said. "I've

been tryin' to fire him ever since Peacock hired him."

"So what's the problem?"

"He's Peacock's brother-in-law."

"That's right, I heard that already," Butler said. "You fellas are trying to buy each other out."

"Say," Masterson asked, "you wouldn't be lookin' to buy half interest in a saloon, would you?"

"Your half?"

Masterson shook his head.

"Peacock's."

"I'm afraid I wouldn't have the money to buy half interest in a place like this. Besides, you don't know what kind of partner I'd be."

"You already kept me alive once," Masterson said. "That already makes you a better partner than A. J. Peacock."

"What about Neal, here?"

"Me?" Brown asked. "I don't have a dime to my name."

"Neal would make a great partner," Masterson said, "but other than the fact that he doesn't have any money, he also doesn't want to own a saloon."

Brown made a face. "Too stable."

"So right now," Masterson went on, "I'm stuck with Peacock."

"And him with you," Butler said, "unless you get killed."

"And you kept that from happening," Masterson said. "I think I see ..."

"You think they were sent to get me out of the way," Butler said, "making you easier to get to?"

"Well, you are staying in town for a while," Masterson said. "With you and Neal watching my back I'll be harder to kill."

"Great," Butler said. As if it wasn't bad enough he was already a target, now he'd have two bull's-eyes on his back.

"You're gonna need somebody to watch your back," Brown pointed out.

"I think I may have the man."

"Who?" Brown asked.

"I can ask Ben Thompson."

Neal Brown and Jim Masterson fell quiet.

"Unless he's not welcome in the Lady Gay?" Butler asked.

"Bat has a lot of respect for Ben," Brown said. "He just doesn't like him very much."

"And you?"

Jim shrugged.

"I guess I don't know him that well."

"So ... I'll talk to him?" He didn't bother to mention that Thompson had sort of already assigned himself that role, anyway—like when they walked back to the Dodge House together the night before.

"Sure, why not?" Masterson asked. "If they're gonna start sending men at us at this rate—twice in three nights—we'll probably need all the help we can get."

Butler hesitated a moment, then asked, "What about your brother? What about Bat?"

"What about him?"

"I mean ... is asking for his help an option?"

"No," Jim Masterson said, "it's not. Bat's in Tombstone with the Earps. He's got his own life, and I've got mine."

"Okay, then," Butler said. "Just so I know. Now I guess all we need to find out is who's sending these men?"

"Peacock," Neal Brown said. "That's why Al Updegraff has lit a shuck."

"Could be," Masterson said.

"What about this whole Dodge City Gang versus Reformers thing?" Butler asked. "I read about that in the newspaper."

"There's no damn Dodge City Gang," Masterson said, "but I wouldn't put it past the new mayor to want to get rid of us, one way or another."

"But he fired you," Butler said.

"And we're still here," Brown pointed out.

"And we're stayin'," Masterson said, "for now."

"I'll talk to Ben, then," Butler said, "and let you know what happens. Meanwhile—"

"We'll keep our guns loaded and ready," Brown assured him.

CHAPTER 34

A. J. Webster's first four days in office had been good, but not completely satisfying. He'd heard what had happened in the Alhambra the first night the gambler, Butler, had been in town, and now there'd been shoot-outs at the Lady Gay, again involving Butler. Both times Jim Masterson had come out alive.

Now Fred Singer was standing in front of the mayor's desk, trying to explain why he had not run Butler out of town.

"It's your job now to keep this town clean, Marshal," Webster said. "We don't need more men like Jim Masterson and Chalk Beeson and Dog Kelley comin' into Dodge, we need less."

"I understand that, Mr. Mayor," Singer said, "and I am doin' my job—"

"Not if that fella Butler is still in town," Webster said. "Sounds to me like if it wasn't for him we wouldn't have Jim Masterson to worry about anymore."

Singer frowned.

"Mayor, you didn't have anything to do with sending those men after Masterson, did you?"

"What? No, of course I didn't."

"Because if you did I'd have to—"

"I told you, I had nothin' to do with it," Webster said, overriding the marshal. "All I'm sayin' is one of our problems could've been solved without us lifting a finger to do it."

"I can't just run Butler out," Singer said. "All witnesses say he drew only when provoked."

"I don't care when he drew," Webster said, slamming his hand down on the desk. "The next time he does, I want you to get him out of Dodge. Is that understood?"

"Yes, sir."

"And I want you to assign a man to the telegraph office."

"What for?"

"I want to know if Jim Masterson sends for his brother Bat—and if he does, I want to know about it right away."

"Yes, sir."

"And what about Ben Thompson?"

"W-what about him?"

"If push comes to shove, which way is he gonna jump?" the older man asked.

"I can't say for sure, Mayor."

"I wish Peacock and that brother-in-law of his would take matters into their own hands already," Webster said. "The two of them are more capable of killin' Jim Masterson than any of these hired guns have been."

"I been wonderin' about that myself, Mayor," Singer

agreed, "If they done it themselves it might be over already."

"That's what I just said."

"I meant to say—"

"Look, Fred," Webster said, "I gave you this job—Jim Masterson's job—because you assured me you could do it."

"Yes, sir, I can, but—"

"Then do it," Webster said, his voice rising. By God, just go and do it!"

Updegraff came back to the Lady Gay, slipped in the back way while Butler and Brown and Masterson were in the saloon. He made his way up the stairs and tapped on his brother-in-law's door. There were some muffled curses from inside and then the door swung open. Peacock stared angrily at Updegraff, who was looking past the man at the woman on the bed. All he could see was her big ass, and it was as red as a beat. He also saw what he thought was the imprint of a hand there.

"Stop staring at Carol's ass, Al. Whataya want?"

"Didn't you hear the shootin' downstairs?"

"Yeah, I did," Peacock said. "I was sort of hopin' our problem was solving itself."

"Well, it didn't. That gambler got in the way again."

"You were supposed to take care of that, Al—"

"I know, but—"

"It was your job."

"I know, Anthony, but—"

"You were supposed to find some men good enough to handle it," Peacock went on.

"Well, he was better with a gun than I thou—"

"Get some talent, damn it!" Peacock growled.

"I'll need more money, Anth—"

"Use what you stole from the other batch of money I gave you," Peacock said.

"I—that ain't enough for more than one ma—"

"Then get one man," Peacock said. "Get one man good enough to do the job, and tell him to make it look like a fair fight—maybe an argument over a poker game, or a woman."

"Okay, but—"

"If we can't get someone to get this done, Al," Peacock said, "you and me might have to strap on our guns and do it ourselves."

"That'd be okay with me—"

"Well, it wouldn't be okay with me." Peacock kept his voice down because he could hear Masterson, Brown, and Butler in the saloon. "Take care of Brown, get rid of Butler, and Masterson will have to stand alone. Got it?"

"Yeah, I got—"

"Good. Then do it." Peacock slammed the door in Updegraff's face before the man could take another good look at the welts rising on Carol's ass.

CHAPTER 35

Ryerson bothered Butler.

It didn't make sense. All the man did was exactly what Butler did that first day for Jim Masterson. He noticed something suspicious going on, followed up, and saved Butler's ass.

Well, he helped him, anyway. He had saved Butler the way Butler had saved Masterson. After all, Jim had killed one of the men from the balcony, and Butler had taken another one. So Ryerson had been helpful, but what he did wasn't lifesaving.

But just the fact that he was there to help didn't feel right to Butler, and he didn't know why. Maybe what he needed to do was talk to the man. What he didn't know was that wouldn't be easy to do.

Ryerson left the Lady Gay knowing he'd done the right thing, even if it had exposed him earlier than he'd planned. He was going to go and have the meal he was looking forward to, and then go to his hotel for some shut-eye. He was going to have to be fresh to be able to do what he had to do.

After Butler left the Lady Gay, Neal Brown looked over at Jim Masterson.

"What?"

"We're gettin' him involved in our affairs," Brown said.

"He got himself involved when he took a hand the other night," Masterson said. "He knows what he's doin'."

"I hope so. I hope we all do."

"What's that mean?

"Why are we stayin' around here, Jim?" Brown asked. "They don't want us here."

"I got a business—"

"Sell it," Brown said. "Sell out to Peacock. Goddamnit, let him have it."

"I can't."

"Why not?"

"I can't turn tail and run just because they took my badge," Masterson said.

"Why not? Bat did. It ain't hurt his rep any."

"I ain't Bat," Masterson said. "I can't be Bat."

"Jim—"

"You can go, Neal," Masterson said. "Any time you want. No hard feelings."

"Naw," Brown said. "Look what happened to Hickok when Charlie Bassett left him alone for too long."

"I ain't gonna get shot in the back, Neal."

"Yeah, you ain't," Brown said. "Not as long as I'm around. So forget it. If you're stayin', I'm stayin'."

"I'm gonna get dressed," Masterson said. "If that

idiot Updegraff comes back, don't let him leave."

"I'll shoot him in the foot if I have to."

As Masterson went back upstairs, Neal Brown moved around behind the bar and got himself a beer.

Ryerson had disappeared.

He wasn't on the street and Butler didn't know what hotel he was staying at. He recalled the man saying he wanted a meal, but he didn't see him in the Delmonico or the Dodge House. He'd have to check into him another time.

Or maybe not ...

When Butler walked into the *Dodge City Times* office M.J. Healy looked at him in surprise.

"Do you have more information on those men?" she asked.

"No," he said, "I'm not interested in the dead, I'm interested in the living."

"Like who?"

"Fella named Ryerson, Kevin Ryerson. Ever heard of him? Read anything about him?"

"No, and no," she said. "Do you want me to do some research for you?"

"What will it cost me?"

"Nothing," she said, with one of those smiles he felt to his toes. "I've got your interview and it's comin' out tomorrow. I'll just do this to try and help you."

"Okay," he said. "That's nice of you."

"It'll cost you another meal," she added suddenly.

"That's a price I can pay," he said. "I'll check back with you later in the day."

"Isn't he the man who helped you?"

"Yes."

"Then why are you asking about him?"

"Because I don't know him, or anything about him," he said. "Why would he help me?"

"Why did you help Jim Masterson that night?"

"Because it was the right thing to do."

"And this Ryerson," she asked him, "his reason couldn't be the same?"

"How many men have you ever know who did something just because it was right?" he asked.

She thought a moment, then asked, "Other than you?"

"Yes."

She thought again, then said, "I'll try to have somethin' for you by this evening."

"I'll be back."

He turned to leave, realized she was alone.

"Where's your brother?"

"I'm wonderin' the same thing," she said. "If you see him tell him to get his sorry ass back here. I need him."

"I'll do it," he said. "See you later."

With Mary Jane Healy doing the research on Kevin Ryerson, Butler went looking for Ben Thompson. He checked his room at the Dodge House but he wasn't there. Neither was he eating there, in the dining room. It was still too early for the saloons to be open for business, so he was at a loss as to where to look for him. He was going to have to settle for catching up to him whenever he could, and hope that his back didn't need watching before then.

CHAPTER 36

When Butler reentered the Lady Gay he found Neal Brown behind the bar, nursing a beer.

"Want one?" Brown asked.

"Why not?" Butler said. "I've already had whiskey for breakfast."

Brown drew him a beer and set it on the bar.

"Where's Jim?"

"Gettin' dressed. Did you locate Thompson?"

"No, I'll talk to him later. I was, however, trying to find Ryerson, but couldn't."

"Why him?"

"Because he came and went so fast," Butler said. "I'd like to find out something about him."

"Like what?"

"Like where he's from. Where he's going and why he stopped to help me? Do you have any idea who he is?"

"No, I never saw him or heard of him before."

"Never saw a wanted poster on him?"

Brown thought a moment, then said, "Not that I

can remember. What makes you suspicious of him?"

"I'm just naturally suspicious of everyone," Butler confessed, "especially when they pop up out of nowhere to help me."

"But that's what you did." Brown reminded him.

"Yeah, but I'm not suspicious of myself."

Brown was confused, but decided not to pursue it any further. He had enough of his own troubles to keep him occupied.

"Neal, what do you think about whatever's between Jim and Bat?" Butler asked.

"I think it's their business."

"If Jim sent Bat a telegram asking for help, would Bat come?"

"In a minute."

"Then why doesn't Jim ask?"

Brown shrugged.

"You'd have to ask him."

"Why don't you send a telegram?"

"Because Jim would kill me if he found out. Besides, there's nothin' goin' on here that Jim and I can't handle—with a little help from you, that is. I mean, the other night."

"I was glad I was there," Butler said, "and I'll help more if something happens while I'm here."

"You know," Brown said, "once you're seen takin' sides, you're gonna become a target."

"It looks like that already happened, doesn't it?"

"Oh, yeah . . ."

"What about guns in town?" Butler asked. "If there's enough to be hired to go against you, what about some being hired to work for you?"

"Jim's not gonna hire any guns, Butler," Brown said. "That ain't his style."

"If he was still a lawman, wouldn't he hire more deputies if he needed them?"

"Well, yeah ..."

"What makes this any different?"

Brown thought a moment, then said, "I don't know, it just is. Don't get me wrong. He'll accept help, like from you or anyone who wants to help. But he ain't gonna go out beggin'."

"I'm not suggesting that—" Butler said, but was interrupted by the appearance of Jim Masterson.

"Suggestin' what?" he asked.

"Butler was just askin' why we don't, uh, enlist some help."

"Enlist? You mean, like pay?"

"I didn't mean—"

"Look," Masterson said, "we lost our jobs and some folks are gonna use that fact to come after us now, when they couldn't do it while we wore badges. That's just somethin' we're gonna have to deal with. It won't last forever."

"Just until somebody's dead, maybe," Butler said.

"Maybe," Masterson said, "but that won't be my choice. Look, Butler, you've helped enough. You don't have to—"

"If I can help more, I will."

"We're even, you know," Masterson said. "After this mornin'."

"What was that about, anyway?' Brown asked.

"I don't know," Butler said. "Could be a carry over from the other night."

"I'm willin' to bet a man like you has got enemies of his own," Brown said.

"That's true enough. Could have nothing to do with you and Jim, at all."

"But we can't be sure of that," Masterson said. "You find Thompson?"

"No, I'll talk to him later." He decided not to go through the whole thing about Ryerson again. Besides, he had Mary Jane Healy trying to find out some information. "What are your plans for today?"

"Me? I'm gonna run my business." He looked the part, his black suit and white shirt matching Butler's.

"What about your bartender?"

"I'll talk to him when he comes back."

"Think he will come back?"

"Oh, he'll come back," Masterson said. "He's arrogant, and he's got his brother-in-law to protect him. He'll be back."

"Well, see if he knows anything about those men that tried for me this morning," Butler said. "It sure seemed to me that he knew what was going on."

"Don't worry," Masterson said. "We'll ask him."

"Okay, thanks."

Butler headed for the door.

"You still interested in an early game?" Masterson called after him.

"Yeah, I am."

"Check back with me later. I may have something for you."

"Thanks.

As Butler left Brown turned to Jim Masterson.

"What do you think of him?"

"He seems to be able to handle himself."

"I mean, are you suspicious of him?"

"What for?"

Brown explained about Butler being suspicious of Ryerson, and why.

"So you're thinkin' we should be suspicious of him?"

"I'm just applyin' his own rules to him," Brown said. "He did pop up out of nowhere and take a hand the other night."

"Yeah, but he also stayed around and ended up gettin' shot at for it," Masterson said.

"Yeah, well," Brown said, "maybe I'll just be as suspicious as he is for a while, until he proves himself."

"He's proved himself to me already," Masterson said, "but you do what you gotta do."

"I always do, Jim."

CHAPTER 37

Ryerson had his meal in a small café off of Front Street and then went to his hotel. Before going to bed he took the wooden chair from the room and jammed it beneath the doorknob, then put the pitcher and bowl on the windowsill, so no one could open the window without knocking it off. Only when he felt he was safe from being surprised did he lie on the bed, his gun belt on the bedpost within easy reach.

He only needed a few hours, because he had ridden day and night to get to Dodge City.

Butler knew he'd only given M.J. a couple of hours to find something on Ryerson, but he was impatient. The man intrigued him, and he wasn't sure why. Maybe he'd just had gunman after him for so long, he had to check everybody out.

When he entered the press was going, manned by M.J.'s brother, Lou. Apparently, he'd managed to find his way to work. He waved, received nothing back, and went into the office where M.J. was sitting at the desk.

"I know, I know," he said, waving a hand, "you need more time—" he started.

"Actually, I don't," she said. "I checked and checked but there's nothing in any western paper about a Kevin Ryerson."

"What about eastern papers?"

"We don't have many—"

"I saw a *New York Herald* in there when I was looking."

"We have a few, but—"

"Good, then it won't take you long to check them?"

She frowned.

"All this for a meal?"

"At the restaurant of your choice."

"Well," she said, "we could go back to your friend Hank's place, but I want this meal to cost you, so I choose the Delmonico."

"You've got a deal. I check back with you later."

"Wait."

"What?" He stopped at the door.

"How about a word about the shooting this morning?" she asked. "Are you sure you didn't know any of those men?"

"Didn't know them," he said, "and never saw them."

"Then, can you see any reason for them to try to shoot you?" she asked.

"This is the West, right?" he asked her. "That's what men out here do, isn't it? Shoot at each other?"

He left quickly, before she could ask another question.

* * *

As Butler came out of the newspaper office he heard his name being called from across the street. He stopped, turned and saw Marshal Fred Singer coming toward him. He waited for the lawman to reach him.

"I'm glad I caught you," Singer said. "Can you come to my office for a few minutes?"

"What for, Marshal?"

"I just want to have a talk."

"Actually, I was just going to—"

"I'm makin' it a request, Butler," Singer said, "but that could change."

Butler hesitated a moment, then shrugged and said, "Well, in that case, lead the way."

Updegraff was heading back to the Lady Gay to talk with his brother-in-law when he was Fred Singer walking with Butler. He watched them just long enough to figure they were going to the lawman's office, then continued on his way at an increased pace.

"Have a seat," Singer said.

The marshal's office was in a two-story brick building. There were several desks for him and his deputies, and the cellblock was on the second floor. It was not typical of any lawman's office Butler had seen in the past.

Singer hung his hat on a wooden peg on the wall and sat behind his desk. Butler sat in a chair just across from him.

"What's this about, Marshal?"

"It's about you, Mr. Butler," Singer said, "and the possibility that you might be takin' the wrong side."

"Am I taking sides?"

"Obviously, you are."

"Oh, I see," Butler said. "Because I saw that someone was going to try to bushwhack Jim Masterson and Neal Brown, and I took a hand to stop it, that means I'm taking sides?"

"In this town, it does."

"You mean this town that has two sides, the Dodge City Gang on one and the Reformers on the other?"

Singer frowned.

"You sound like you've been readin' back issues of our newspaper," he said.

"And does that put me on one side or the other?"

"Let's not talk about sides," Singer said. "Let's just talk about what's right for you."

"And what would that be?"

"I'd say that would be to move on."

"No room for another gambler in Dodge? Or will you be telling Ben Thompson to move on as well."

"Ben will move on, eventually."

"And so will I."

Singer paused, then said, "Maybe I should just make this a suggestion."

"All right."

"I suggest you don't use your gun again while you're in Dodge," the lawman said. "You've killed enough men here."

"Is there a quota?" Butler asked.

"I don't know what that means," Singer admitted. "I just don't want to have to take your gun and put you in a cell."

"You won't have to."

"Good."

"I won't kill anyone who isn't trying to kill me," Butler said. "How is that?"

"Is that the best I'm gonna get out of you?"

"Best I can do, Marshal," Butler said. "I'm sure not going to take a bullet because you don't want me to kill another man. I'll kill anyone I have to in order to stay alive."

Butler stood up, stared down at the seated man.

"That I can promise you."

"I can understand that," Singer said. "That's personal. Just don't be takin' on anyone else's problem while you're here."

"Is that another suggestion?"

"Let's make that a piece of advice."

"I didn't know giving out advice was part of your job, Marshal," Butler said.

"It's a new service offered by the marshal's office," Singer told him.

"I'll see what I can do."

Butler turned to leave, stopped when he got to the door.

"These other desks."

"Yes?"

"Have you hired your deputies yet for your new office?"

"Don't worry," Singer said. "I've got deputies."

"Enough of them?"

"Enough to do the job," Singer said. "Why? Are you thinkin' of takin' on a new profession?"

"Oh, no," Butler said. "I'm very happy with the one I've got. I was just ... curious."

"Good day, Butler," Singer said. "I hope we won't have to talk again."

"Oh, I hope that, too, Marshal," Butler said. "I surely do."

CHAPTER 38

Butler decided he needed a quiet place to think, maybe over a cup of coffee. He knew the perfect place—which, he realized, still didn't have a proper name.

When he got there it was empty, as usual, though as he entered he smelled something cooking in the kitchen. Despite the fact he'd had a big breakfast, he suddenly became very hungry. Might have had something to do with the fact that he'd already downed whiskey and beer before lunch.

"Hank?" he called.

When there was no answer he decided to go ahead and stick his head into the kitchen. He saw Hank sitting on the trunk that held his gun belt, and who knew what other remnants of a past life.

"Hey, Hank."

The man started, looked up at him without really seeing him for a moment, then seemed to come to.

"Oh, hey, Butler."

"What's wrong?" Butler asked, coming into the kitchen. "You don't look so good."

"I, uh, I had a customer this mornin'."

"Well, that's good, isn't it?" Butler asked. "I mean, kinda good."

"You know," Hank went on, "I thought having a small café I'd be able to cook, feed some people, and nobody would recognize me. It worked pretty good for a while."

"And?"

"This mornin' a man came in, sat down and had a meal."

"And he recognized you?"

"No," Hank said, "that's just it. He didn't recognize me. I recognized him."

"Oh," Butler said. "Well, was it someone you think might recognize you later on and come back?"

"I'm not sure," Hank said. "I mean he might come back, and if he does he might want to try me."

"And then you'd either have to put your gun on again or let him kill you."

"Right."

"Well, what are you going to do?"

"I don't know," Hank said. "I been sittin' here thinkin' about it."

"Is this somebody I'd recognize if you told me his name?" Butler asked.

"I ain't sure," Hank said. "You ever hear of a man named Kevin Ryerson?"

"You saw what?" Peacock asked.

"I saw the marshal taking Butler into his office."

"So?"

Updegraff stared at his brother-in-law, who was seated

at his desk in the back office of the Lady Gay. There was a second desk in the room that belonged to Jim Masterson but—up to now—had rarely been used.

"So I thought it would be important."

Peacock sat back in his chair.

"Al," he said, "I'll tell you what's important and what's not. What the hell happened this mornin'?"

"That Gambler came over lookin' for an early game and Sandland and his partners made a try for him."

"They tried to kill him?"

"Well ... yeah."

"Did you tell them to do that?"

"Anthony," Updegraff said, "you said you wanted me to get rid of him so he couldn't help Masterson."

Peacock covered his face with one hand.

"I didn't tell you to have him killed," he said. "I wanted you to get rid of him! Get him out of town."

"Well," Updegraff said, defensively, "I thought when you said get rid of him—"

"Never mind," Peacock said. "Look, Jim is lookin' for you, so's Neal Brown."

"What for?"

"They want to see what you know about this mornin'," Peacock said.

"So what do I do?"

"Stay out of sight for a few hours. Come into work later as if nothin' happened. And if they ask what you know, just play dumb." Peacock hesitated, then added coldly, "That should be real easy for you."

Butler and Hank sat down with a huge pot of coffee.

"He's a bounty hunter," Hank complained, "but a real

low-key one, you know? Keeps to himself. His reputation is only with those people who know him."

"Well, I never heard of him," Butler said. "I've got the newspaper editor here trying to find something out about him."

"She won't," Hank said. "He don't get ever written up in newspapers."

"So where do you know him from?"

"I saw him twice," Hank said. "Both times I thought he was after me, but he wasn't."

Hank had just told Butler that he was not only hiding from his own reputation, but that there was a price on his head as well.

"I watched him work, those two times. Brought both men in dead. He give them a choice. They drew and he killed 'em."

"Faster than you?"

"I never said I was fast."

"Any man cares for his gun the way you do, even after you've put it down, wasn't slow."

"Okay," Hank said, "so I was fast, but faster than Ryerson? I never wanted to test it."

"Where's he from?"

"Who knows," Hank said. "I only know a couple of places where he's been. I seen him in Montana, and once in New Mexico."

"He gets around."

"He goes where the money is," Hank said. "If the price is high enough, he goes for it."

So the price on Hank was high enough that, on two occasions, he thought Ryerson was after him.

"So do you think he's after you now? After you've put your gun away all this time?"

"Who knows?" Hank asked. "Could be a lot of men in Dodge City he's after."

"I wonder if he'll check in with the marshal?"

"He's a legitimate bounty hunter," Hank said. "My guess is he would. He'd want to make sure the man had the funds to pay him."

"Unless he expects to be paid on the other end."

Hank paused for a moment, thinking. Butler assumed he was wondering if the bounty hunter could kill him here, or if he'd have to take him back to wherever it was they put the price on his head.

Butler believed in second chances. Hank—*whoever* Hank was—had hung up his gun and started over. He didn't think he should have to worry about a bounty hunter collecting a price that had been set years before.

And then, of course, there was the possibility that Ryerson was there for Tyrone Butler.

CHAPTER 39

Butler told Hank his story.

"My father had political affiliations in Philadelphia that got him and the rest of my family killed. He saved me by sending me west. He told me that no matter what happened, I should never come back."

"And you haven't?"

Butler shook his head.

"How long?"

"Almost ten years."

"And is Butler your real name?"

"Yes."

"But ... why not change it, if you're on the run and hidin' out?" Hank asked.

"Because I'm not hiding out," Butler said. "I won't give up my name. If they want to try to collect a price on my head, let them come."

"So, whoever killed your family ..." Hank said

"A man," Butler said, "a political faction or party? ... I'm still really not sure."

"They still have a price on your head?"

"Apparently. The last time I know for sure they tried was Wichita—a couple of weeks ago. And then this morning, at the Lady Gay, somebody tried ..."

"Somebody?"

"Yeah," Butler said, "we're not sure if they were after me for me, or because I helped Jim Masterson the other night."

"When you do somethin' like that," Hank said, "you're definitely takin' sides."

"That's what the marshal just told me today."

"A couple of weeks ago the Masterson side might have been the right side, but since the election ..."

"Yeah, I get that, too."

"So you gonna move on?"

"No," Butler said. "I came here to do some gambling and that's what I'm going to do. What are you going to do?"

"About Ryerson?" Hank shrugged. "I don't know. I definitely don't want to go on the move again. I guess I'll just have to wait and see if he recognized me. The fact that I'm supposed to be dead might put him off some."

"And then what?"

"Well ... to tell you the truth I'll face him, but only because of the story you just told me."

"My story? Why?"

"I admire that you won't give up your name," Hank said. "Mine ... well, if I told you, you might not come and eat here no more, so I'll still keep that to myself, but if Ryerson comes after me, I'll just have to make a stand."

"I think that's a good plan," Butler said.

"Well, I wish I could say the same for yours. If I was you, I'd saddle up and get the hell out of Dodge."

"I appreciate the advice, Hank," Butler said, "but I'll go when I'm good and ready."

"Well, you want somethin' to eat while you're waitin'?" the man offered. "On the house."

"Can't turn that down, can I?"

"Steak?"

"With all the fixin's?"

"Comin' up," Hank said, and went back to the kitchen.

While he was gone Butler wondered about this man who was believed dead. He wondered how he was supposed to have been killed, but didn't want to ask. There were things they had both held back about their stories and wouldn't want to be asked about. Maybe, when Hank was good and ready, he'd tell Butler the rest of the story. As for Butler, he'd just keep the rest of his own story to himself a while longer.

CHAPTER 40

Butler had a meal fit for a king. Seems it paid to confide your secrets once in a while. His only worry now was whether he would be able to eat with M.J. later that evening at the Delmonico. For that reason he turned down Hank's offer of pie and coffee.

"Listen," Hank said, as Butler was leaving, "my gun's in the trunk, but if you need some backup you let me know."

"You'll be a little rusty."

Hank grinned.

"It ain't somethin' you lose, Butler," he said. "Not when it comes naturally. I was a dead shot when I was fifteen. You just say the word and I'll strap it on. I ain't got many men I can call a friend, I don't wanna lose one."

Butler shook the man's hand and said, "I'll call on you if I need to, Hank and you do the same, hear?"

"I hear ya."

"I don't know many men who can cook a steak as good as you," Butler added. "I don't want to lose one."

* * *

The time between meals went quietly for Butler. He returned to his hotel and had a long, hot bath and a haircut, so he'd look presentable when he picked M.J. up for their supper.

When she answered his knock at her front door, she did not look happy.

"I'm sorry," she said, "I didn't find out anything about this man, Ryerson."

"That's all right," he said. "I did."

"What? How?"

"I'll tell you once we're seated at the Delmonico."

He needed the extra time to think about what he could tell her. He didn't want to give away Hank's secret, but then decided that Hank really didn't have to be anyone other than a plain old cook who had seen Kevin Ryerson before.

The Delmonico was busy, but they were able to get a table easily. M.J. was greeted by other diners; it seems that most townspeople knew her.

They stopped at one table and she said, "Hello, Mr. Mayor."

"Miss Healy," the new mayor said. He was in his forties, overweight, wearing a suit and checked vest, dining with his wife, who was middle-aged but handsome.

"Mayor and Mrs. Webster, allow me to introduce my friend Tyrone Butler."

"Your ... friend, dear?" Mrs. Webster asked, with a twinkle in her eyes.

"No, Ma'am," M.J. said, "not that kind of friend. Well, enjoy your meal."

"And you," Mayor Webster said.

On the way to their table she said, "And that was our new Mayor, A. B. Webster."

"Why do so many people in Dodge just use initials, and not their names?"

As they were seated she said, "You know, I guess I never noticed that, but you're right."

"Seems to me it would be a lot simpler just to have a mayor named Dog Kelley."

"You're right."

"How did he get that name, anyway?" Butler asked. "Dog?"

"Racing dogs," she said, "He used to own and race them and now that he's not in office, maybe he'll go back to it."

"A form of gambling I haven't discovered," Butler said. "I guess I'll stick to poker and an occasional horse race.

A cute, young waitress came over and greeted M.J. by name."

"Holly, this is Mr. Butler."

Butler noticed this time she left off the "my friend" part. Wouldn't want people to continue to get the wrong idea.

They both ordered coffee. M.J. ordered an expensive steak dinner. Hank's steak was still on Butler's mind, if it wasn't weighing heavily on his stomach. He ordered beef stew.

"So tell me," she said, placing her chin in the palms of her hands, with her elbows on the table, "how did you hear about Ryerson—and what did you hear?"

"He's a bounty hunter. A good one, but not a very well-known one—by choice."

"And who told you this?"

"Hank did."

"And how does he know?"

"He recognized him from a time when they were both in Montana," Butler said.

"So he's a bounty hunter, and he's just passing through?" she asked. "And he decided to help you out of some trouble, even though there's no money in it for him? Doesn't sound like any bounty hunter I ever knew. They don't usually do anything if there's not a bounty in it."

"I know," Butler said. "Makes me even more curious."

"Me too," she said, "about whether or not he's here on business, or is just passing through."

"Ask him for an interview," Butler said. "Maybe you'll be the first to get one. I understand you're very persuasive, that way."

"You know," she replied, "I might just do that."

CHAPTER 41

Over dessert M.J. told Butler about her desire to work for a newspaper in a big city.

"San Francisco," she said, "Chicago, New York. That's where I see my career going."

"And how are you going to get there?" he asked.

"There will be a story," she said. "One story that will take me there, I know it."

"What kind of story?"

"That I don't know," she said, "but I will know it when I see it."

It seemed to Butler that the big stories in Dodge City had been ten years ago. Still, he hoped that it would happen for M.J. With her looks and her drive, he knew she'd go far if she made her way to the big city.

"When we did your interview—which ran today, by the way—you said you were from the East."

He hadn't said what city he was from, and he was hoping she wouldn't ask now.

"Have you ever been to New York?"

"Oh, yes," he said, "and Cleveland ... and Chicago."

"Where else?"

"Big cities?" he asked. "That's it, I guess. I'm going to make my way to Denver and, eventually, I'll get to San Francisco. I'm looking forward to gambling in Portsmouth Square."

"It sounds so exciting."

"I think it will be."

"Can I ask you something?"

"Sure," he said, "Since the interview is already in print—you'll have to give me a copy."

"I will," she promised. "What I want to ask you is, with all that's happened here, with three men trying to kill you this morning ... why would you not just leave Dodge City? Go directly from here to San Francisco?"

"It's not just about going to San Francisco," he replied. "It's about the whole journey. I've seen a lot to this point, and done a lot, but there's more to see between here and California."

"I suppose," she said, "but as soon as I have a chance, I'm leaving here and going right to San Francisco."

He reached across the table and touched her hand. "You'll fit right in there."

"Will *you*?" she asked.

"In San Francisco? Oh, yes," he said. "That's a talent I have. I can fit in anywhere."

"It must be nice to be so confident," she said.

"You're confident."

"I seem confident," she said. "I'm really not, though. That's my secret. I've been scared ever since my parents died. And I have Lou to worry about."

"Will you take him with you to San Francisco?"

"I honestly don't know," she said. "I don't think he'd fit in there. He's more suited to living here."

"Would he want to go with you?"

She hesitated, then said, "I think so."

"Have you talked to him about it?"

"Oh, no," she said, shaking her head. "He knows nothing about my ambitions. He thinks I'm very happy here."

"It will come as a shock to him, then," Butler said. "Maybe you should start preparing him now."

"I probably should," she said, shaking her head, "I just don't know how to."

"Shall I walk you home?" he asked.

"I'm sorry," she said. "Here I am chattering on and you probably want to get to work. You said that in your interview, right? That poker is your work?"

"Yes," he admitted, "I did say that."

As they stood up she said, "Let's stop by the office first and I'll give you a copy of today's edition, with the interview."

"All right."

Butler paid the bill and they left the Delmonico.

They stopped at the office to get him a copy of the newspaper and then he walked her the rest of the way home.

"Thank you for the meal," she said, in front of her house, "and the time."

"It was my pleasure."

He took a step forward and impulsively kissed her cheek.

"Please don't slap me," he said, backing up. "I just wanted to do that."

"I won't slap you," she promised, "but then don't you be shocked at me."

She stepped forward, put her arms around his neck and kissed him on the mouth, softly but soundly.

"I just wanted to do that."

She blushed before he could say anything, turned and hurried into the house. He touched his hand to his mouth, then smiled, turned, and walked back to Front Street.

He did, indeed, have to go to work.

Kevin Ryerson was shocked when he woke up and saw what time it was. For him to have slept that soundly and that long was unusual. He figured he must be getting old.

He poured some water into a basin and used it to wash his face and torso, scrubbing the gumminess from his eyes and the trail dust from his chest and armpits. After that he dug out a clean shirt and put it on, then checked his gun to make sure it was in good working order. In all the years he'd been a bounty hunter he'd never suffered a misfire on any of his weapons, and this was the reason why. He always checked his weapons before he went out into the street. If he was on the trail, he checked it every morning when he woke up.

When he slid the gun into the holster and strapped it on, he was ready to go outside. His other meal seemed like a distant memory. He wanted another steak, and then a couple of cold beers. Maybe even a woman. He had no work to do tonight. His target was here, and he could wait until tomorrow to go after him. He'd ridden hard to get here and deserved some down time.

He left the room and went down to the lobby, thought briefly about going into the dining room, but then decided to treat himself to the most expensive restaurant in town.

He stopped at the front desk to ask the desk clerk just where that would be.

CHAPTER 42

Butler stopped by the Lady Gay to check in with Jim Masterson and Neal Brown. The place was busy, almost completely full. He saw Updegraff behind the bar, but didn't approach him. Instead, he scanned the room, spotted Brown, and walked over to where the man was watching a poker game. He stopped next to him. There were five men at the table and he didn't know any of them.

"Butler," Brown said.

"Neal. I see the bartender came back."

"Jim questioned him," Brown said. "He swears he doesn't know anything about what happened this morning."

"What else would he say?"

"That's what Jim said."

"Where is Jim?"

"Upstairs. Should be down soon. He took supper in his room."

"Oh."

"Had one of the girls up there with him, too," Brown

added. "I think he was tryin' to relax a bit. Didn't have much time to do that when he was wearing a badge. You ever find that early game?"

"No, never did. Stopped looking, actually. Had other things to do. Why, did Jim get one going?"

"This was it, actually," Brown said. "Saved a seat for you as long as they could."

"Doesn't look like they missed me much."

Brown looked at him. "They got by."

"Well, tell Jim I'm sorry I didn't get back here."

"Where are you off to?"

"The Alhambra, I think."

"You see Dog, tell 'im we'll be over in a bit."

"I'll do that."

"Oh, ever find Thompson?"

"No," Butler said. "Stopped looking. Figure I'll see him when I see him."

"And Ryerson?"

Butler, who had half turned to leave, turned back and told Neal Brown what he had found out about Ryerson.

"Interesting," Brown said, when he'd finished. "I wonder if he's here for somebody in particular, and if so who?"

"That's the question."

"Maybe one of us will get a chance to ask him."

Butler thought he should probably also tell Brown about his conversation with Fred Singer, but he was anxious to get over to the Alhambra, so he left that for later.

* * *

If the Lady Gay was busy, the Alhambra was just about bursting at the seams. There didn't seem to be room at the bar for another body, but he wanted a beer. He was trying to decide when to make a space for himself when he noticed somebody waving him over.

It was Kevin Ryerson.

Butler only hesitated a second, then walked over to the man, who was smiling.

"I thought that was you," he said. "You want a beer?"

"Sure."

Ryerson leaned in and shouted at the bartender. A moment later he leaned out and handed Butler a frothy, cold beer.

"I was wondering where you disappeared to this morning," Butler said. "I don't know that I thanked you properly for helping me."

"I had to get some sleep," Ryerson said. "I rode pretty hard for two days to get here."

"Some reason you had to get here in a hurry?" Butler asked.

Ryerson sipped his own beer and nodded.

"Business."

"What kind of business is that?"

Ryerson's eyebrows went up.

"You don't know? I thought for sure you'd know by now. Figured you'd check me out."

"There's not much to check," Butler said. "Apparently, you keep a pretty low profile."

"Well, in my business—you know what business I'm in, right?" he asked.

"Bounty hunter."

"Right. In my business I think too many of my colleagues make a point of gettin' their names out there. They make their reputations as important as the money."

"And you don't do that."

"Hell, no," Ryerson said. "To me it's all about the money. That's the only reason I do it. I don't relish the hunt, or the kill if it comes to that. Just the money."

"So the money is the only reason you do it."

"I just said that—but no, wait. The reason I can make my money this way is that I'm good at it. So I guess I do it because I can't see any other way to make the same money. Must be the same with you. You're a gambler, right?"

"Right."

"You know any other way you can make the same money?"

"No."

"And you do it for the money, right?"

"I enjoy it," Butler said. "I do get a thrill out of it."

"Well," Kevin Ryerson said, "it sounds to me like we got a lot in common."

"Not the least of which is we're both in Dodge City at the same time," Butler said.

"Do you believe in coincidence?" Ryerson asked.

"I've seen too many of them not to."

"I don't," Ryerson said. "I think everything happens for a reason. You, me, those men this morning, we were all there for a reason. Anyone know who they were, by the way? Or why they wanted to kill you?"

"Not why they wanted to kill me," Butler said, "but somebody identified one of them as a fella named Red Sandland."

"Red Sandland," Ryerson repeated, frowning. "Can't say I know him. If there was paper out on him I'm sure I'd remember. I have a memory for that kind of thing. Faces, too. I remember faces."

Butler wondered if Ryerson had remembered Hank's face yet.

"So, are you here on business?" Butler asked. "Or just passing through?"

Ryerson drank some beer before answering, regarded Butler over the rim of his glass. His eyes looked amused.

"I never talk about my business, Mr. Butler," he said, lowering the glass. "Let's say I was here looking for you. Well, word might get around, you'd hear about it, and then you'd run—or try to shoot me in the back. Not that I'm sayin' you'd do that, but some folks might try to bushwhack me rather than run. My point is—"

"You don't talk about your business," Butler finished for him. "I got it."

"Good. No offense?"

"No offense."

"So are you here to gamble? Poker, is it? Or something else?"

"Poker, usually," Butler said, "but it looks real busy in here tonight. I might try over at the Long Branch."

"Hey, I wanted to take a look over there, too. Mind if I walk over with you?"

Butler eyed the man. Was he just trying to get him outside, on the street?

"I don't mind," he said, "but I'm not ready to leave just yet. Why don't you go over—"

"Hey, I'll wait," Ryerson said. "Still got to finish my beer. And you owe me one, right?"

"Right," Butler said. "I'll return the favor at the Long Branch."

"No problem," Ryerson said. "Just give me a sign when you're ready and we'll mosey over."

"Right," Butler said. "I'll do that."

Ryerson nodded, still looking amused at something—or was his smile more mocking than amused?

Butler took his beer with him and moved away from the bar.

CHAPTER 43

Butler moved through the crowded saloon until he came to a setup of three poker tables, all completely filled. Off to one side he noticed Dog Kelley, but rather than watching the game the man looked like he was just staring off into space. Butler sidled up next to the man and waited to be noticed.

"Oh, Mr. Butler," Kelley said finally. "I'm sorry, I'm afraid I was ... somewhere else."

"I've been there, Mr. Kelley," Butler said. "Sometimes it's a better place."

"And sometimes not," Kelley said. "And I thought I asked you to call me Dog."

"Dog, it is. Have you seen Ben Thompson tonight?"

"I haven't," Kelley said. "I was thinkin' he might have left town."

"Really? I had breakfast with him and he didn't say a word about that."

"Maybe I got it wrong, then," Kelley said. "He's probably gambling over at the Lady Gay, or the Long Branch tonight."

"I was at the Lady Gay and he wasn't there. I'll give the Long Branch a try."

Kelley turned his body so that he faced Butler.

"If you're lookin' for a game, I can set up a table for you. I'm sure we can get some more players."

Butler looked at the men who were manning the three tables and said, "No, I don't think so."

"Believe me," Kelley added, "I can make sure you have a level of competition you're comfortable with."

"I appreciate that," Butler said, "and I might take you up on it later, if that's okay."

"That's fine," Kelley said. "I'll accommodate you any time. I've also beefed up my security here, so I don't think you'll have to worry about a repeat of what happened this morning."

"That's good to know," Butler said.

He was tempted to ask Kelley if there was a back way out he could use, but decided against it. If Ryerson was in Dodge looking for him, he'd have to face it, soon enough.

"Well, I better be going. Oh, Neal Brown asked me to tell you that he and Jim Masterson would be over a little later on."

"Good," Kelley said. "I haven't seen either of them all day. Obliged for the message."

Butler made his way back through the crowd and found Ryerson waiting by the batwing doors.

"Didn't think you'd be much longer."

The man seemed good-natured as they came, but Butler suspected it was an act. They were about the same age, but Ryerson was clearly a man of the West. His clothes were clean, but they wore trail clothes, and his gun was well taken care of.

They left the Alhambra and headed down the street to the Long Branch. It was dark now and they were guided by both the brightness of the place and the noise. They could hear Chalk Beeson's five-man orchestra playing, and somebody was trying to sing above the din.

As they entered, Butler realized that the Long Branch was the premier drinking, gambling establishment in town. While there were at least sixteen saloons in Dodge, they all provided one or two services, while the Long Branch provided everything and more.

"Quite a place," Ryerson said, as they stood inside the batwing doors.

They moved over toward the two-piece cherrywood bar and managed to elbow into place just opposite the two stuffed golden eagles that Beeson kept behind it. They managed to find a place at the bar only because the Long Branch was bigger than the Alhambra, and had more room.

"Two beers!" Butler shouted to the bartender, who nodded and set them up. They were ice cold.

"That ain't the cowboy band I heard so much about," Ryerson said, eyeing the orchestra.

"No," Butler said, "I heard that Beeson is out of town right now with the band."

They had to either shout to be heard or lean in close to each other.

"I want to check out the gambling," Butler said.

"Go ahead," Ryerson said, raising his mug. "I don't gamble. I'm good right here."

"See you later."

"Thanks for the beer."

Butler waved off the thanks. He was only repaying the beer he'd had at the Alhambra.

He moved through the crowd. There had to be more people here than at the Alhambra, yet it was easier to get around. It wasn't only that it was bigger, but it seemed to have been laid out with more thought given to gamblers and drinkers.

Butler found his way to the tables, which were running blackjack, roulette, red dog, chuck-a-luck, and poker. Off to one side he saw Trixie dealing at her faro table.

The poker tables were in full swing, most with house dealers. One table did not have a house dealer but was playing dealer's choice, and Butler was not surprised to find Ben Thompson sitting right there, in the midst of all the action. He was in the middle of a hand—which he ultimately won—and while raking in his chips he looked up, locked eyes with Butler, and nodded. Butler returned the nod. Thompson raised his eyebrows, as if to ask "Are you gonna play?" and Butler made a gesture as if checking a pocket watch, then raised his beer, as if to reply, "In a while, when I finish this."

Butler took his beer back over to the faro table to watch Trixie deal for a while. She was wearing a gown that was even lower cut than last time, and her creamy breasts seemed ready to spill out, even more so when she would take a deep breath—which she seemed to do at strategic times. Butler knew that Wyatt Earp and Doc Holliday dealt faro, and had probably dealt it here, but they certainly did not have Trixie's God-given advantage.

He watched as men approached the table, kept their heads bowed, then turned and walked off as she took their money. At one point she saw him and graced him with a smile even while she was shuffling the cards. Her hands were amazingly dexterous and he watched them with fascination, wishing he could handle cards that well. He wondered just how talented she was with the deal, whether it be faro or poker.

He felt someone come up beside him. It was Bill Harris, part owner of the Long Branch.

Suddenly the music stopped and it was much easier to talk.

"Glad to see you back."

"She's very good, isn't she?" Butler said.

"She's the best I ever saw," Harris said, "and I saw Doc Holliday deal."

Butler took a sip of his beer, realized he was down to the bottom of his mug.

"Another one?" Harris asked. "I can have a girl bring it over."

"No," Butler said. "Thanks, I'm done drinking."

"Time to gamble, then?"

Butler had forgotten how annoying Bill Harris had been the last time he was there, but on the other hand he had won a lot of money, so the place felt lucky to him.

"I think so."

"Want to try Trixie?"

"Faro's not really my game."

"Poker, then?"

"Poker," Butler confirmed.

Harris took his empty mug and handed it to a passing girl.

"This way," he said.

Butler almost told him he could find it himself, but thought better of it. If there was a question about who got an empty seat at one of the tables it couldn't hurt to have Harris on his side.

"Lead the way, Bill."

CHAPTER 44

The first empty chair was not at Ben Thompson's table, which suited Butler for the moment. Thompson would want payback for the last time they played, and Butler preferred to build up a stake before that happened. If Thompson took money from him he wanted it to be money he'd taken off other players on this night.

He was at a table with a house dealer, and the game was five-card stud. There were five other players and the dealer quickly reeled off their first names. Butler would remember some, but it was over the course of the game that they'd all become people to him. He'd also come to recognize who his competition was—and who the sore loser was.

In this case his main competitor was a man named Corbin, who looked like a drummer but was actually a professional gambler. He was in his forties, fancied expensive cheroots and didn't drink while he played.

The sore loser was a man in his thirties named Lane. In his thirties he kept drinking whiskey, and the more he drank the looser he played. The looser he played, the more he lost. And the more he lost, the more some of the players rode him. This was a welcome change from the last time, when there was a man riding Ben Thompson the whole time. Here, while there was the potential for fireworks, at least they wouldn't involve flying lead. While Lane was wearing a gun, it looked like a weapon that would more than likely blow up in his hand when he tried to fire it. Clearly he was not a man who used his gun often.

The other three players were just there to pass the time, and were donating money to Corbin's cause until Butler sat down. After half an hour Butler could see that he had caught the attention of Corbin and the two men acknowledged each other. Slowly, their piles of chips began to grow as the others dwindled. After a while men came and went, and their names were not important to Butler.

Oddly, Lane stayed in the game. He made outlandish bets, and every so often he'd win a big pot, giving him enough to stay in.

It didn't matter who came and went at the table, they all seemed to know who Lane was. Butler discovered that he was married, owned a small business in town—apparently, a hardware store—and that his wife hated when he played poker because he usually lost. Everyone seemed to know that, and it was the crux of most of the jokes.

And they all called him "Lane," so Butler didn't know if it was his first name, or last.

A couple of hours into the game Lane was so drunk his face was fiery red and he didn't seem to be able to see his cards. He also constantly had trouble lifting the edge of his hole card so he could peek at it—which he did a lot.

But he seemed to have a hand he liked a lot, and soon he and Corbin were left alone to play it.

With four cards dealt Corbin had received a three, a nine, and an ace. Lane got two eights in a row, then a king. He bet the eights like they were aces or as if he had another in the hole. Butler doubted that he had another, and could see that Corbin felt the same way. Every time Lane bet, Corbin raised, which frustrated Lane.

The fifth card came out. Corbin bought a three and Lane a useless four. Butler could see the writing on the wall. He figured Lane for eights, and he thought they'd hold up. As for Corbin, Butler thought he'd been raising to annoy Lane, and also because he had a pair of threes. As far as Butler was concerned, the man now had three threes, and Lane was beat.

But Lane didn't see it that way.

"Two hundred," Lane said, making his largest bet of the night.

Without hesitation Corbin said, "Raise two hundred."

"Goddamnit!" Lane slurred. "Every time I make a fuckin' bet, you raise the same damn amount."

Corbin only shrugged.

"The play is to you, sir," the dealer said.

"I know the fuckin' play is to me," Lane shot back. Butler could see it coming. Bad players always ended up this way.

"I got ..." Lane stopped to count his chips, had to

start again twice—probably because he was seeing double—and then said, "six hundred and forty dollars left. That's my bet."

If the man was seeing double Butler wondered if he thought he had four eights.

"Six hundred and forty?" Corbin said. "All right, Lane. I'll call."

"You can't beat my eights," Lane said, turning over his hole card triumphantly, "and my fours." His useless four had not been so useless after all.

"Actually," Corbin said, "I can," and turned over his third three.

"Three threes," the dealer said. "The winner."

"N-no, wa-a-ait," Lane stammered. "T-that's all my money."

"Then you shouldn't have bet it," Corbin said, raking the chips in. "Looks like you're busted. I'm sure there's someone waitin' for your chair."

This was the most Butler had heard Corbin say all night, and now he detected a slight Southern accent.

"No, no," Lane said, "I c-can't go home without my m-money. My wife'll kill me."

"Here," Corbin said, tossing a five dollar chip over to the man. "Buy her somethin' nice."

The gesture incensed Lane, and Butler could see what was about to happen. He also knew that Bill Harris had some security in the place, though none of them were anywhere near the table. If he didn't do something, somebody was going to end up dead. It seemed to him that this kind of thing was starting to happen at every game he played in.

He was seated to the left of Lane, who was left-handed, and thus was wearing his gun on his left hip. The man made a clumsy attempt to pull the gun, and Butler knew that Corbin would kill him if he did. Butler quickly leaned over and snatched the gun from Lane's holster.

"Wha—" Lane blinked, looked at Butler. "Gimme my gun!"

"Lane," Butler said, "I think your wife would be even madder at you if you got killed tonight."

Butler grabbed a passing girl by the arm and asked her to get Bill Harris.

"Yes, sir."

Lane stood up and demanded belligerently, "Gimme my damn gun!"

Butler turned the weapon over in his hand, saw how old and dirty it was.

"Lane, this thing would take off your hand if you tried to fire it." He quickly emptied it, pocketed the shells and then handed it back to the man. Immediately, Lane began to fumble with the shells on his gun belt, trying to reload the weapon.

"Is there a problem here?" Bill Harris asked, appearing at Butler's elbow.

"Yes," Butler said, "if Lane succeeds in reloading his gun he's going to end up getting killed."

"I'll take care of it."

Harris waved and two men appeared on either side of Lane. Each man grabbed an arm and removed him from the table.

"Hey, wai—" Lane shouted. "I gotta get my money."

"They'll take him outside and get him some air," Harris said to the table. "Please, keep playing."

The dealer looked around and said, "Do we still have a game, gents?"

A man sat down in Lane's chair, and was just as interested in the answer as the dealer.

"We have a game," Corbin said. "Deal."

CHAPTER 45

After two hours the players began to dwindle so, once again as it had happened the night before, they consolidated the tables. Butler ended up sitting with Corbin, Ben Thompson, and two other men.

Corbin was a steady professional, but once he ended up at a table with both Ben Thompson and Butler he started to lose.

"Gents," he said, eventually, standing up, "I think I better get out while I still have a few dollars. Mr. Butler, I'd be honored to buy you a drink when you're done here."

"Be my pleasure, Mr. Corbin."

"Gentlemen," Corbin said, touching the brim of his hat.

He passed behind Butler and out of sight.

"I believe that man's a bigger fool than I thought," Ben Thompson said.

"Why's that?" Butler asked.

"He's takin' the rest of his money over to Trixie's faro table." Thompson laughed.

"He'll lose the rest of it there," Butler said.

The other men at the table laughed. Twenty minutes later they were gone and Butler and Ben Thompson were laying head-to-head again. Both were significantly ahead for the night.

"If you don't mind," Thompson said diplomatically, "I'm not exactly in a winner-take-all frame of mind to-night."

"That suits me."

"Besides," Thompson said, gathering up his chips, "your luck is runnin' too damn good tonight. I know better than to buck a man's string of luck."

Butler actually attributed his winning to skill more than luck, but decided not to argue with Ben Thompson about that.

"Who's your friend?" Thompson asked.

"Who?"

"That feller's been watchin' you all night." Thompson jerked his chin and Butler looked in that direction. He saw Kevin Ryerson standing where he could easily see the poker table.

"Has he been there all night?" he asked.

"Ever since you sat down," Thompson said, then, "no, since Lane got carried off. I guess that attracted his attention."

Butler frowned, annoyed that he had not noticed the man himself.

"He's not a friend," he said, "he's a bounty hunter."

"Who's he after?"

"He won't say if he's even after somebody," Butler said.

"Well, can't be me," Thompson said. "I've got no price on my head, that I know of."

Butler realized that his silence was saying more than he ever could, but decided to maintain it.

"Drink at the bar?" Butler asked.

"I have a previous appointment with a lady," Thompson said, as they stood up. "Perhaps next time. Besides, Corbin's waitin' at the bar to buy you one."

Butler looked over at the bar where Corbin was standing.

"I guess he left Trixie's table with some money after all."

Butler and Thompson started to walk away from the table and were confronted by Bill Harris.

"Done for the night?"

"Yes, we're done, Bill," Thompson said.

"I'll have those chips cashed in for you, gents." He waved two girls over.

"I'll just go with the little lady and cash them myself, Bill," Thompson said, "but Butler, here, has somebody waitin' for him at the bar."

"Just give your chips to Heather, Mr. Butler, and she'll bring you your cash at the bar."

Butler hesitated, then said, "All right," and handed the pretty, chubby brunette his chips.

"Don't waste any time, Heather," Bill Harris told her. "Mr. Butler will be at the bar."

"No, sir."

"Thanks, Bill," Butler said. "Maybe I'll see you to-morrow."

Butler walked over to the bar, leaving the saloon owner standing in the middle of the floor.

"Beer or whiskey?" Corbin asked.

"Beer."

While they waited he noticed that Ryerson was standing at the other end of the bar. Was he just trying to make Butler uncomfortable?

"There ya go," Corbin said, handing Butler his beer.

"Thanks." Butler sipped. "How did you do at the faro table?"

"The dealer was too beautiful for me to concentrate," Corbin said. "I lost a few dollars and gave up. Then I asked her to have a drink with me, but she told me she didn't fraternize with the patrons. How did you do?"

"I did all right."

At that point Heather appeared and handed Butler a thick sheaf of bills. He took one out and handed it to her.

"Thanks, Mister."

As Butler tucked the money away inside his jacket, Corbin said, "Looks like you did more than all right."

"You seemed to have left ahead," Butler said.

"Just about," the other man said. He was taller, more slender than Butler and—like Butler and Ben Thompson—was wearing a dark suit. "I was cleanin' up until you came along, and then things got worse when we moved to Ben's table. It was time for me to go."

"What's on your mind?"

"Sorry?"

"You said you wanted to buy me a drink. I thought you might have something on your mind."

"Not really," Corbin said. "I just admire the way you handle yourself at the table. You know your way around a deck of cards."

"Well, thanks ..."

"You also did me a favor, keeping me from killing that sore loser, Lane."

"I didn't see that it would do anyone any good," Butler said. "In fact, if I was you I'd be careful when I left here. He might be hanging around outside."

"I'll keep that in mind. By the way, who's the fella at the end of the bar? He keeps watchin' us. He was watching' us play, too."

Butler wondered if everybody in the Long Branch was more observant than he was.

"His name is Ryerson," Butler said. "He's a bounty hunter, and I don't know what he's doing here."

Corbin's mug hit the bar with a bang that startled Butler.

"A bounty hunter?" Corbin asked.

"Yes. Do you know him?"

"No," the other man said, looking distracted, "no, I don't know him ..."

"I can introduce you—"

"No!" Corbin snapped. "Uh, no. Truth is I, uh, hate bounty hunters. I'm gonna turn in, Butler. Good night."

Corbin headed for the door and Butler noticed that he gave Ryerson a wide berth. He also noticed the bounty hunter looking after Corbin until the gambler disappeared through the batwing doors. Seeing that Butler was alone, Kevin Ryerson picked his beer up from the bar and walked over to him.

"Hey, I watched you play tonight," he said. "You're very good. I could never tell when you had a hand and when you didn't."

"I get the feeling you'd be a good poker player, Ryerson," Butler said.

"Who me? No, I couldn't take all the tension—you know, waiting to see what the other players have? That's not for me."

Once again Butler saw amusement in the man's eyes, and he didn't like it. Suddenly, he didn't want to be around the man.

"I think I'm going to turn in, Ryerson."

"Where are you staying?" Ryerson asked him. "I'll walk back with you."

"The Dodge House."

"Wow. Expensive hotel."

"I like to stay in nice places."

"Me, I watch my money," Ryerson said. "Stay in the worst places. Can I walk with you?"

"Actually, I'm waiting for Ben Thompson," Butler lied. "He's staying there, too. We're going to walk together."

"That's a good idea," Ryerson said. "You never know when somebody's gunnin' for you, you know? Like some bad loser? It's good to have a man like Thompson watchin' your back."

"Yeah, it is," Butler said.

"Well then," Ryerson said, setting his mug on the bar next to the one left by Corbin, "guess I'll head on back to my rat trap of a hotel. Maybe I'll see you tomorrow."

"Yeah," Butler said, "maybe you will."

Ryerson smiled, touched the brim of his hat and said, "Thanks for lettin' me hang around you."

"Maybe we learned a little something about each other," Butler told him.

"I believe you're right, Butler," the bounty hunter said. "I believe you're right."

Ryerson turned and left the Long Branch without a look back. Butler wondered which of them had learned more?

CHAPTER 46

Butler stepped through the batwing doors and stood in front of the Long Branch Saloon. Corbin was gone, Ryerson was gone, Ben Thompson was gone. It was quiet on the street—too quiet to suit him. Dodge City should never be this quiet.

The only time towns like this were this quiet was when everybody knew that something was about to happen. Of course, this late at night there wouldn't be many people on the street, anyway. It was just late, the saloons would close soon, and people had gone home.

He had an itch in the center of his back, like somebody had a gun trained on him.

Ryerson annoyed him. If the man was there for him, why didn't he just get it over with? And if he was after him, why did he help him against Sandland and the other two? Was it the money that was on his head? Hell, he could have collected it, anyway.

And Corbin, his entire attitude had changed when he found out that Ryerson was a bounty hunter. Did he have a price on his head? Was he thinking Ryerson might have been in Dodge looking for him?

Butler turned and started walking in the direction of the Dodge House. He decided to have it out with Ryerson tomorrow. If the man wanted to play a game of nerves, Butler didn't have the time to indulge him. He couldn't concentrate on poker and Ryerson at the same time. He'd managed it tonight, but Ben Thompson had been right. As skillfully as he played, he'd had a good run of luck the past couple of days. But most of the time he depended on his skill, and for it to work for him he had to give the game all his attention.

But what would he do—what should he do—if he found out that the bounty hunter was in Dodge for Hank? Warn him, sure, but back his play? He hadn't known the man very long, but long enough for Hank to confide in him—sort of. And long enough for him to tell Hank his own story.

No, there was no way he could just throw Hank to Ryerson.

And there was still Jim Masterson and Neal Brown. They had probably been watching each other's backs for years. Did they really need him? Well, the other night they had. If not for him at least one of them would probably be dead.

But Butler's game was poker, not gunplay. His skill with cards led him to believe he was not really gambling. Gambling meant there was a chance you could lose. At the poker table he might come up short one night, but in the long run he always won.

When it came to guns, though, that was Butler's gamble. So far he'd been able to handle himself every time, but when would his luck run out? When would they finally send enough men after him that he wouldn't be able to handle?

Halfway to the Dodge House he stopped short and listened. If somebody wanted to take him, now would be the easiest of times. In the dark. He'd never seen it coming. He waited, muscles tensed in case he had to move. Maybe the first shot would miss, and he'd be able to react. It had happened before.

When he was sure it wasn't going to happen he continued on, and eventually he made it to the safety of the still lit lobby of the Dodge House Hotel.

Kevin Ryerson watched from the darkness as Butler walked to his hotel. He'd enjoyed the game he'd play that evening with Butler, but tomorrow the games would be over. He'd have to do what he came to Dodge City to do.

Once Butler entered the Dodge House, Ryerson turned and did what he'd told Butler he was going to do. He headed for his own hotel for the night. As he walked, though, he replayed the scene where the other gambler walked by him in the Long Branch. He'd heard him called Corbin by someone, but that name didn't fit the face, not in his mind. He couldn't put his finger on it, but he knew him. The question was, did he know him because there was a price on him? Ryerson was always up for a little extra work if it meant a lot of extra money.

Tomorrow, he thought, he'd work it out tomorrow.

* * *

When Corbin got back to his room he poured himself a whiskey from a bottle he kept in his saddlebags. He didn't know Kevin Ryerson, had never seen him before, but he new the type of man he was. The type who had gunned his older brother down years ago because of a two hundred dollar bounty. Bounty hunters always brought those memories back for him, and he knew it'd be in his dreams that night, too. But in the safety of his room, maybe enough whiskey would keep him from dreaming.

Butler locked his door, removed his jacket and his gun belt. He sat on the bed and took a deep breath. All he wanted was to be left alone to play poker. Why couldn't he have that? He'd almost convinced himself that he would never go back to Philadelphia. There was nothing he could do to bring his family back, and he still didn't know who had killed them, or had them killed. Not directly. He knew it had to do with his father's politics, though.

On a couple of occasions he'd managed to keep alive one of the men who tried to kill him for the money. He asked them who sent them, but they never knew. All they knew was that there was a lot of money waiting for the man who killed him. He'd let one of those men go, and he had come back at him a second time, almost succeeding. He killed him, and after that he learned his lesson and killed them all.

Maybe one day somebody would get the message, and it would all stop. Until that time he lived as well as he could on jacks and queens and stayed alert.

CHAPTER 47

When Butler woke the next morning it was a beautiful day. From his window he could see that the sky was clear, the sun was out, everything looked fresh and clean— well, as fresh and clean as it could look in Dodge City. Buckboards and horses kicked up enough dust to choke a horse, but that was to be expected. All things considered it was a fresh, new day and anything was possible.

He dressed and left his room for breakfast. As he did a door opened further down the hall and Trixie stepped out. She didn't see him and headed for the stairs, looking a bit rumpled but beautiful, in the same dress she'd worn last night. As he passed the room she'd come out of he saw that it was Ben Thompson's.

"Good for you, Ben."

He took breakfast in the hotel dining room again, eating alone this time. Ben Thompson did not come down the entire time he was there. He probably needed some extra rest this morning, which Butler could well understand.

He still had not had a chance to talk to Thompson about the possibility of watching each other's back while they were in town. There were just too many possibilities now: Ryerson, somebody who didn't want him to help Masterson and Brown or—if the bounty hunter wasn't there for him—somebody else trying for that payday.

He stepped outside, looked up and down the street. Normal hustle and bustle, the kind that a man could easily get lost in if he didn't want to be seen.

Butler decided to take it easy today. He looked around, found a straight-backed wooden chair and sat in front of the hotel, watching the morning go by. On a rare occasion he'd smoke a cigar, and this morning he felt like one. He nabbed a boy of about ten going by and promised him a quarter if he'd go to the general store and buy a couple of cigars.

"What kind?" the boy asked.

"The kind that are three for a nickel will do." That way the boy wouldn't run off with the nickel if he knew he was getting a quarter for making the purchase. "Get me three of them and I'll give you your quarter."

"You got a deal, Mister."

He gave the boy a nickel and sat back in his chair to wait.

The man known as Hank opened his trunk and stared down at the gun and holster. It had been part of his life for such a long time that even now, when he had convinced himself that he'd put it down for good, he couldn't get rid of it. And now with Ryerson in town he might have to put it back on, or die.

And what about Butler? Should he really have trusted him? What if he went to Ryerson? No, he wouldn't do that. He wasn't that kind of man. If it came down to it he'd be able to trust Butler. He'd back the gambler, and the gambler would back him. Of that he was sure.

He closed the trunk and went to fire up the stove.

The gambler Corbin woke and wondered if he ought to quit Dodge. There were opportunities to make money, but there were also opportunities to get killed.

One really wasn't worth the other, was it?

Ryerson woke in a bad mood. His tongue tasted bad, his head ached, and he wished he'd spent money the night before on women, not on beer and whiskey.

He washed quickly, but took his time over his ritual with his guns. He did his pistol this morning, and his rifle. Before the day was out he'd probably need both.

He went down to the street, found a small café—a different one than last time—and had breakfast. Halfway through his meal he remembered two things.

He remembered that Corbin, the gambler, had a price on his head in Missouri.

And he remembered who the café owner was from the day before.

Suddenly, Dodge City was a treasure trove of bounty money. All he had to do was figure out how to go about getting it all.

A. J. Peacock went to the telegraph office first thing in the morning and sent off a telegram he hoped would solve all his problems. He was tired of counting on idiots like his brother-in-law and the man he hired. He knew Updegraff was probably keeping some of the money he'd given him to hire men, which was why he'd been hiring stumblebums instead of men who were good with their gun.

So Peacock finally decided to open his purse and dig down deep to get the job done.

Jim Masterson was up earlier than most. In fact, he'd slept very little that night. He kept turning over in his mind Neal Brown's words about selling and getting out. It just rankled him that people would think he left Dodge City with his tail between his legs. What he would rather do was get his money for his share of the Lady Gay and then leave town at his own leisure.

But who was he kidding? What he really wanted to do was get his badge back.

Over a cigar Butler realized that Dodge City was a powder keg. There were just too many guns there. Maybe it wasn't like the old days when the Earps and Bat Masterson and Bill Tilghman and Charlie Bassett were around, and maybe it wasn't the volatile situation he'd heard existed in Tombstone at the moment, but it was bad enough that he decided to send a telegram. They needed somebody in Dodge with the ability and the balls to put things right.

He thought he knew just who that would be, but he needed to word the telegram very carefully.

He walked to the telegraph office after breakfast, but stopped short when he saw a man coming out. Butler hadn't really met A. J. Peacock formally yet, but he knew the man on sight; and Jim Masterson's partner was coming out of the telegraph office, looking both ways as if worried someone would see him.

Butler waited across the street until Peacock satisfied himself that he wasn't being watched, and slunk away. Only then did he cross the street and enter the office himself.

"Help ya?" the middle-aged clerk asked. He wore a visor and sleeve garters, like he could have been dealing faro as much as sending telegrams.

"Was that A. J. Peacock who just left here?"

"Yes, sir," the man said, "but don't go askin' me what he was doin' here. I ain't allowed to talk about it."

"Not even if I ask you real nice?" Butler asked, taking out some money.

"Put your money away, friend," the man said, waving with both hands. "It'd be real nice to have, but my job is nicer, and I got a family to feed."

"Okay, then," Butler said, satisfied that the man wouldn't talk about his telegram, either, "I've just got two lines to send myself."

CHAPTER 48

With the telegraph message sent, Butler decided to go back to his chair in front of the hotel. This seemed preferable to trying to find something to do while waiting for the saloons to open and the poker games to get underway.

Of course, he could always take Bill Harris up on his offers to arrange a game for him, but he found that he didn't care for the man and did not want to be indebted to him. He was satisfied with the games he'd been playing, even if they were not particularly challenging to him. So far Ben Thompson had been the only real competition, and, thanks to his run of luck, he had taken the man's measure. His real competition, he felt, would come when he finally made his way to Portsmouth Square, in San Francisco.

He took out another three-for-a-nickel cigar and lit it, enjoying both the smell and the crackle of the cheap tobacco. He nodded to men who entered the lobby, tipped his hat to the women with them, and tried his best to relax. So far the gambling had been going well—and when you really looked at it, the gunplay had gone well, too. He was alive, he was ahead of the game.

"Got another one of those?"

He looked up at Ben Thompson and said, "Three-for-a-nickel cheroots don't seem to be your style, Ben."

"Or yours."

"I'm going cheap."

"I'll go along with you," Thompson said. "Just let me get myself a chair."

He went into the lobby, came out with a rather nice-looking armchair that belonged in the lobby, not out on the walk. Of course, no one was going to stop Ben Thompson from taking whatever chair he liked. It could even have been the lobby divan.

He sat next to Butler, accepted the cigar and a light, then drew deeply.

"Jesus, you're right," he said, "this is cheap."

"If it's any consolation, I paid a kid a quarter to fetch them for me," Butler explained.

"Ah, three for thirty cents. That does sound better."

"I notice you had company last night."

"Saw her leavin' this mornin', did you?"

"Just by coincidence."

"She's a fine woman," Thompson said. "Very talented."

Butler didn't respond.

"No, I mean, she's talented with a deck of cards."

"I didn't say anything."

"It's what you were thinkin'."

"Now you read minds?"

"If you can't read minds sometimes," Thompson responded, "you shouldn't be playin' poker. You read minds very well at the table. That's how you know when to call and when to fold."

Butler didn't think of it as mind reading. He thought of it as having good instincts and being able to read people.

When he didn't respond to Thompson's word, the other man changed the subject.

"There's somethin' goin' on in this town," he said.

"Like what?"

"I thought you'd know that better than I do. All I know is, I can feel the tension."

"Well," Butler said, "I can tell you what I know, but there's a whole hell of a lot I don't know."

"I can start with what you know."

Butler told him . . .

"I got a question," Thompson said when Butler finished.

"What?"

"Why would you get involved?"

"I reacted to the moment," Butler said. "I saw two men obviously casing the Lady Gay from outside. I saw them check their weapons. I figured they were up to something and it wasn't good. What would you have done?"

"I just got to town like you did?" Thompson asked. "I would have gone to my room and got some rest."

"And just let whatever was going to happen play out?"

"You betcha."

"Okay," Butler said, "say you were inside, at the bar, and you saw these two jaspers going for their guns."

"Not my business," Thompson said. "I've never understood why some people want to get involved in something that just ain't their business. You'd be havin' a lot less trouble right now if you'd kept to yourself, wouldn't you?"

"Probably."

"Unless ..."

Butler didn't rise to the bait.

"Unless," Thompson continued, "those three fellas the other mornin' were after you for another reason."

Butler remained silent.

"Maybe the same reason that fella Ryerson's in town?"

Butler let Thompson continue uninterrupted.

"But then why would Ryerson take a hand to help you?" the other man asked. "To save his bounty? But if you were dead he could probably have collected it himself."

Thompson fell silent for a moment, puffed on his cheroot.

"But you've asked yourself these questions already," he said, finally. "I'm just repeatin' them. Is this helpin' you figure anything out?"

"Not particularly."

"Well," Thompson said, regarding the glowing tip of his cheap cigar, "I guess I can do what I can to help keep you alive."

"Why would you?" Butler asked. "That wouldn't be mindin' your own business."

"You've got some of my money," Ben Thompson said, turning to look at Butler. "I can't win it back if you're dead. That makes it my business."

"Yeah, right," Butler said.

"You sayin' you don't want my help?"

"No, no," Butler said, "I'll take it. Doesn't matter to me how you justify it."

"So, you want to go and ask that bounty hunter what he's doin' in town?" Thompson asked.

"I was thinking about it," Butler said. "But there's more."

"How much more?"

More than he was going to say. He wasn't going to give Hank up, but he did mention how disturbed Corbin seemed to be to find out that Ryerson was a bounty man.

"So, he explained that," Thompson said. "He told you he hated bounty hunters."

"That Corbin has a price on his head and that's why he was bothered?"

Butler shrugged.

"Okay, so maybe Ryerson recognized him," Thompson said. "Or maybe he's the reason Ryerson is here, and you got nothin' to worry about."

"Why's he hanging around me, then?"

Thompson smiled, shrugged his shoulders, and said, "Maybe he likes you."

Butler ignored him.

"He's too damn pleased with himself about something," he said. "Thinks he's got something over me."

"Like what?"

"I guess I should find out," Butler said.

"Push him into makin' a move?"

"If he's got a move to make," Butler said.

CHAPTER 49

Ryerson ranked his targets first, second, and third, according to the price he'd get for them. If he'd listed them according to reputation, they would have been in a different order, but his job was about money, not reputation. The only problem he faced was that once he grabbed the first one, the other two would be alerted. On the other hand, once he grabbed the first one—especially if he was forced to kill him—the other two might think they were safe.

He left his hotel carrying his rifle and wearing his pistol, both cleaned to within an inch of their lives and in perfect working order. He headed for Front Street, and his first payday.

Butler and Thompson were crossing Front Street when they saw Ryerson coming their way. They noticed a hitch in his stride when he saw both of then, but then he came ahead. Both men were experienced enough to see the tension in the man, and to feel it in their own muscles. One wrong twitch could cause a bad result.

"Just the man I was looking for," Butler said.

"What a coincidence," Ryerson said. "You're first on my list, Butler."

"You have a list?" Thompson asked.

"That's right," Ryerson said, "and you're not on it, Thompson—unless you choose to be."

"You little pissant—" Thompson started, but Butler broke in.

"No need to get Ben involved," Butler said. "Just for the sake of curiosity, Ryerson, who are the other two?"

"Why do you care?"

"You're not the only one to ask me that lately," Butler said.

"'Care will kill a cat'," Ryerson said. "I think that was Shakespeare."

"Actually, Ben Johnson got there before Shakespeare," Butler told him.

"What the hell are you two talkin' about?" Ben Thompson asked.

"Playwrights," Butler said.

"Jesus," Thompson said. "You're both too damned educated for me. If you're gonna shoot at each other, do it and be done with it."

"Is that what we're going to do, Ryerson?" Butler asked.

"Here's my problem, Butler," Ryerson said. "The price on you is dead only. The other two are wanted dead or alive."

"Why not take them first?' Thompson asked.

"The price here is higher," Ryerson told Thompson.

"I'm curious now," Thompson said. "Why would you

even take on a dead-only bounty? Isn't that close to legal murder?"

"Especially since this bounty is private," Butler said. "It's got nothing to do with the law."

"I don't know anything about that," Ryerson said.

"You don't know who's putting up the money?" Butler asked.

"No idea," Ryerson said. "I got a contact back East who gives me information—the only information I care about."

"The price," Thompson said.

"Exactly. Ready to do this, Butler?"

"Right here? On the street?"

"It's as good a place as any."

"This ain't legal."

Ryerson smiled.

"My contact says I won't have a problem with that. Are you gonna take a hand here, Thompson? 'Cause I gotta say, that would change my order. I'm not foolish enough to take on the two of you at the same time."

"So you'll just move on to the next name on the list?" Thompson asked.

"That's the plan."

"Then I'm in," Thompson said, "so you'll just have to move on."

"Have it your wa—"

"No," Butler said, "wait. I can't do that." He looked at Thompson. "I can't just send him on to the next man. It's not right."

"What the hell's right got to do with it when you're dealin' with a bounty hunter?"

"I'm sorry," Butler said, "I just can't do it." He looked at Ryerson. "Let's do this, just you and me."

"You this good, Ryerson?" Thompson asked. "You always do this face-to-face?"

"I'm not a back shooter, if that's what you mean."

"That makes you a man among bounty hunters, I guess," Thompson said. "I'll just wait over here until you're finished, Butler. I'll buy you a drink to celebrate."

"Same offer apply to me, Thompson?" Ryerson asked.

Thompson ignored him and moved away from the two men.

"Come on, Butler," Ryerson said. "Let's do this before the street gets too busy. One of us might get trampled."

"I still got some questions, Ryerson."

"I told you, I don't know who put up the—"

"Not that," Butler said. "The other two."

"Oh, them," Ryerson said. "I thought I recognized one of them last night, but it didn't come to me until mornin'."

"Corbin?"

Ryerson nodded.

"He's wanted in Missouri," he said. "Small price, but I'll take it. He's third on my list."

"And who's the other one?"

"Ah," Ryerson said, "baggin' this man would add to my rep, if I cared about that. He's supposed to be dead already, so seein' him here was a surprise."

Hank, Butler thought, it had to be Hank.

"But I think I'll keep that to myself," Ryerson said.

"Just on the off chance you kill me, you might decide to go after the bounty."

"You couldn't be more wrong."

"We'll see."

Ryerson set his rifle down against a post and stepped into the street.

"Let's do this," he said. "I've got a long day."

"What's goin' on?"

Thompson turned to see who had asked the question, saw the badge before he saw the man.

"Marshal."

Fred Singer looked over at Butler and Ryerson.

"Who's that talkin' to Butler? It doesn't look friendly."

"It ain't," the gambler said, "in the next few minutes one of them is gonna kill the other."

"What?" Singer asked. "Not in my town."

Singer took one step and Thompson said, "I wouldn't."

"Why not?"

"It's between the two of them."

Singer looked at him.

"Are you tellin' me not to interfere?"

"Marshal," Thompson said, "I'm just givin' you a friendly warnin'."

"Who's play are you backin', Thompson? Must be Butler's. You think he's gonna come out of this alive? Looks like gambler versus gunman to me. You better let me stop it."

"This is what they both want, marshal," Thompson said. "I think you and me just better butt out."

Singer eyed Thompson warily. He knew the man was both gambler and gunman.

"If I try to stop them," he asked, "will you stop me?"

"Let's not find out."

Ryerson backed into the street, his hand down by his gun. Butler stepped down, brushed his jacket back over his holster. Oddly, he thought it was refreshing to find someone who was coming right at him and not trying to bushwhack him.

Ryerson seemed very confident, not a trait Butler liked in a man he was facing with a gun.

Butler did what he did when he was trying to read a man's face to determine what he was holding. He trained his eyes on Ryerson, concentrated, and waited for him to make a move.

Ryerson was thinking about one of his other targets as he faced Butler. He wasn't sure he'd be able to take him the way he was taking this gambler. Corbin, the other gambler, would probably be easier than this, but he'd have to come up with a plan for the third man.

Nobody on the street realized what was happening until the two men drew and fired.

CHAPTER 50

Ben Thompson handed Butler a cold beer.

"Congratulations," he said. "That's quite a move you have."

"I don't think I should be congratulated for killing a man."

"Look at it this way," Thompson said. "You saved the other two men he was after. Did you get their names?"

Butler hesitated just a moment, then said, "No, he wouldn't tell me."

"Doesn't matter, I guess," Thompson said.

"What did you say to the marshal?" Butler asked. "I thought I was on my way to jail for sure."

"I ... reasoned with him," Thompson said. "Made him realize it was somethin' personal between you and Ryerson, and none of his business."

"Well, whatever you said, I appreciate it," Butler said. "At least I didn't have to deal with the law over this."

"He's probably back at his office looking through his wanted posters," Thompson warned.

"That's okay," Butler assured him. "He won't find anything."

"Ryerson seemed to think he was covered," Thompson said. "Might pay for you to leave town, Butler."

"I don't think so." Butler looked down into his beer.

"Was one of the other men Corbin?"

Butler looked at Thompson.

"How did you know that?"

"He skipped town," Thompson said. "I saw him leavin' in a hurry. If he'd just waited a little longer ..."

"Probably doesn't matter," Butler said. "Somebody else will recognize him at some point."

"How often have you had to go through this?"

"Plenty of times," Butler said. "At least this one had the decency to come right at me."

"Yeah," Thompson said, "one of the decent bounty hunters."

They were in the Lady Gay, being served by a bartender other than Updegraff. At that moment Neal Brown came through the batwing doors and spotted them.

"I heard what happened," he said, joining them at the bar. "What was that about?"

Thompson looked at Butler, obviously wondering what his explanation was going to be.

"I have some things to take care of," he said. "I'll see you later, Butler. Brown."

"Thompson."

The two men nodded to each other and Ben Thompson left.

"I guess I never asked," Butler said. "About you, and Jim and Ben Thompson."

"We know each other," Brown said. "Not friends. Bat never liked Ben's brother, Billy. It's ... complicated."

"Isn't everything in this town?"

Brown looked at the bartender and signaled for him to bring a beer.

"You don't have to tell me what this morning was about," he said to Butler. "Not if it's none of my business."

"It was ... personal."

"I know Ryerson was a bounty hunter," Brown said. "I don't hold it against you if there's paper out on you."

"There isn't," Butler said. "Not in the legal sense, anyway. There's ... a price on my head, it's been there a long time, but it's got nothing to do with the law."

"Wow," Brown said, "that is personal, isn't it? You got somebody mad enough at you to put a price on your head?"

"And rich enough to make it a high one."

"So the other morning ..."

"... might have been about that, it may not have been. Today was definitely about that."

"Did he tell you who it was?" Brown asked. "I mean, who put up the money?"

"He said he didn't know."

"Do you believe him?"

"Yes, I've heard that from others."

"Others," Brown said. "How many others have there been?"

"Many," Butler said. "Dozens. I've lost count."

"How long has this been going on?"

"Years ..."

"Jesus," Brown said. "That's like bein' on the run ... and not knowin' who you're on the run from. At least wanted men know they're wanted by the law. That can't be an easy way to live."

"It isn't," Butler said, "but I don't have much of a choice."

"Is Butler your real name?"

"Yes."

Brown held up his hand.

"Okay, I don't need that explanation," he said. "I'm sure you're keepin' your name for a good reason."

Butler was about to say so when Jim Masterson came down the stairs. He looked around at the three or four customers the Lady Gay had at that moment, then joined Butler and Neal Brown at the bar.

"I heard shots while I was getting' dressed," he said to them. "Anyone know what was goin' on?"

"Why don't you get a beer from your bartender," Butler said, "and I'll tell you a story."

CHAPTER 51

Jim Masterson listened to Butler's story—the same one he'd told Neal Brown, with no deviation. Masterson listened while quietly sipping his beer and when Butler was finished he said, "We sure are drinkin' a lot of beer for breakfast since you came to town."

"Really?" Butler asked. "I thought since you owned a saloon that would be kind of ... common."

"No," Masterson said, "I'm more used to eggs." He put his beer down, only half finished. "Probably time for you to leave town."

"Why's everybody telling me that?" Butler wondered.

"You've got enough problems of your own without getting' involved in ours," Masterson said.

"I can make my own decisions, Jim," Butler said. "Besides, there's still some money to be made, here."

"The way I hear it you're doin' all right," Brown said.

"I could do better."

Masterson scratched his jaw.

"You had Thompson out there backin' your play?" he asked.

"All he did was keep it fair."

"But he'll watch your back?" Brown asked.

"Surprisingly, yeah."

"Well," Masterson said, "you couldn't have anyone better—according to Bat, Ben's the best man he ever saw with a gun."

"Bat Masterson said that?" Butler asked.

"Yes, he did," Masterson said. "I don't know that I agree, but he's still a good man to have on your side."

"We agree on that," Butler said. "Ben says he thinks this town is about to erupt."

"He's a pretty damn good judge of the situation, if you ask me," Neal Brown said. "I think Peacock and Updegraff are gonna try to kill Jim outright, any day now."

"I don't think they have the gumption for that," Masterson said.

"I think you're wrong, Jim," Brown said, "but I guess we'll have to wait and see who's right."

"I got some work to do in the back," Masterson said. "I'll see you gents later."

As Masterson went into his office Brown said, "I'll have to stick around him, I think."

"I think you're right," Butler said. "Neal, what do you think about sending for Bat?"

"I'd be for it," Brown said, right away, "but I'd never do it."

"Why not?"

"Well, even if it kept Jim alive, our friendship would

probably be over. He'd be mad as hell at anyone who did that."

"I see."

"Thinkin' about it?" Brown asked.

"No," Butler said after a second, "I can honestly say I'm not thinking about doing it, at all."

Butler left Brown at the Lady Gay and walked over to Hank's café. He found the man in the kitchen, cooking.

"Thought you ought to know," he told him. "Ryerson's dead."

"Who killed him?"

"I did. He came after me first."

"First?"

"Said he had a list," Butler said. "I was first, Corbin was on it, and there was a third man."

Hank took a deep breath.

"He didn't say who the third man was?"

"No."

"You think it was me?"

"No way for me to know that."

"Who's Corbin?"

"Just a gambler, made a mistake a while back, got a small price put on his head. Ryerson had a memory for that sort of thing."

"If that was true, then he probably remembered me, eventually," Hank said. "He'd have to have a helluva memory, though. It's been awhile."

"Doesn't matter now," Butler said. "He's dead."

"Better for everyone, I guess," Hank said. "You hungry?"

Butler shook his head.

"I had breakfast," he said. "Might come back for lunch, though."

"That'd be okay," Hank said. "Thanks for bringin' me the word."

"Sure."

After Butler left Hank tossed a look over at the trunk where his gun was. The leather of the holster was getting old, even though he oiled it. The gun was in good working order, but after all these years, was he? Maybe he wouldn't have to find out.

When Butler got back to Front Street he ran into M. J. Healy, who was hurrying along and stopped short when she saw him.

"Well, thank you very much," she said, although her demeanor was not a very angry one.

"What'd I do?"

"It's what you didn't do," she said. "I had to hear it from someone else that you were involved in a shooting this morning."

Butler shrugged.

"I didn't think it was big news."

"That you shot and killed a bounty hunter on the street?"

"In a fair fight."

"Okay," she said, "but who was he? What was he doing in town? And how did it come to be you who shot him?"

"All very good questions."

"And will you answer any of them?"

He thought a moment.

"I don't want my name in the paper again," he said finally.

"Did you read the interview?"

He hadn't. The paper was still in his room, unopened.

"The man's name was Kevin Ryerson," he said. "He was a bounty hunter. I don't know who he was here for, but he forced me into a confrontation for some reason."

"And you're not wanted by the law?"

"I'm not."

"No wanted posters out on you?"

"No," Butler said. "You can ask the marshal. I understand he was checking on that."

"Maybe I will," she said.

"Don't be so mad," he told her. "There was nothing that happened this morning that's going to get you to San Francisco any faster."

"So are you a gunman now?" she asked. "I thought you were just a gambler. Are you another Ben Thompson?"

"Definitely not another Thompson," Butler said. "I'm not a gunman. The bounty hunter just wasn't as fast with a gun as he thought he was."

"Well," she said, "that was good for you."

"Yes, it was."

"Why didn't the marshal step in and stop it? Or the sheriff?"

"I can't answer those questions," he said. "I don't even know who your new sheriff is."

She was breathing as fast, or looking as agitated as she had been. And she'd never really been angry. Just frustrated.

"Look," he said, "I promise you, if I kill anybody else you'll be the first to know."

"That's not funny," she said, then added, "but all right."

They stood there facing each other for a few seconds, and then he said, "Well."

"Yes," she said, "I have to get back to work. You're, uh, not leaving town because of this, are you?"

"No," he said, "not leaving town."

"Well, good, maybe we can ... talk later."

He smiled at the fact that she had suddenly become very shy.

"I'll come over and see you."

"That would be nice."

She turned and walked away. He watched her for a block, then went his own way.

CHAPTER 52

"When are we gonna make our next move?" Updegraff asked A. J. Peacock.

"As soon as the men I sent for get here."

"Men? How many are we talkin' about?"

"As many as we need to do the job."

"How much is that gonna cost?"

"What do you care, Al?" Peacock asked. "You're not paying anybody anything. In fact, you've made money off all of this."

"What? How?"

"Oh, come on," Peacock said, shaking his head. "Don't make me tell you, Al."

"Are you callin' me a thief, Anthony?"

"What if I am?"

The two men faced each other over Peacock's desk, his face turning red and Updegraff's jaw thrust out pugnaciously.

"Look," Peacock said, "step back and take a deep breath. All we have to do is wait for Ruger and his men."

"You sent for Ruger?" Updegraff asked. "That's gonna cost—oh, never mind."

"Right, never mind," Peacock said. "Whatever it costs is gonna be worth it when I'm sole owner of the Lady Gay."

"Sole owner?" Updegraff asked. "You mean I ain't gonna be your partner?"

"I've had it with partners," Peacock said. "What I'll do is cut you in for a small piece. Let's start with ten percent, minus whatever you've stolen in beer, whiskey, and cash."

"That ain't fair!"

"Stop stealing from me and maybe it'll get fair, Al," Peacock said. "Just do your job for a while until Ruger gets here and then we'll see what happens. Got it?"

"Yeah, yeah, I got it."

"Then go to work."

Updegraff headed for the door, but Peacock stopped him by calling his name.

"What?"

"Keep your gun clean," Peacock said.

"What for?"

"I hired Ruger, that's true," Peacock explained, "but we're gonna get our hands dirty, too."

"That's fine with me," Updegraff said, "as long as I get to pump some lead into Masterson."

"Oh, yeah? And what'll you do when his brother finds out?"

"I ain't afraid of Bat Masterson."

"I'll remind you that you said that, Al, when the time comes."

Updegraff left the office, slamming the door behind

him. Peacock sat back in his chair, laced his fingers behind his head. If Al Updegraff thought he was going to take on another partner after he rid himself of Jim Masterson he was in for a big surprise.

Once Jason Ruger got to town, Jim Masterson's days were numbered, because Ruger didn't let anything get in his way when he was doing a job he was getting paid for—not even the law.

Butler was not happy about having to kill Ryerson. His only consolation was that it had not been a circus. Word was spreading, but they hadn't had a big crowd watching them.

He always felt relieved when he killed a man who was trying to kill him, but he never felt satisfied. Killing a man was not something he enjoyed, even though he had been forced into getting good at it.

He stopped at the general store and picked up three more three-for-a-nickel cheroots. He was going to sit in front of the hotel again, relax, keep his back to the wall, and wait for the poker games to get started in the saloon. Tonight he might try the Alhambra. It would be nice to play without having Ryerson looking over his shoulder.

He settled back into his chair—the armchair Ben Thompson had brought out from the lobby.

Marshal Fred Singer entered Mayor A. B. Webster's office and neither man was very happy.

"That gambler killed a man on the street, Marshal," Webster said. "He should either be in your jail, or run out of town."

"In order to do that," Singer said. "I would have had to go up against Ben Thompson. How would you like to try that, Mayor?"

"It's not my job to do it, Marshal," Webster argued, "it's yours. That's what you get paid for."

"You want my badge?" Singer asked. "Is that what you want?"

Webster sat back in his chair and said. "Fred. Close the door, sit down and calm down."

Singer did as he was asked, but he was still fuming.

"I got word that Peacock has sent for some ... assistance," Webster told him.

"What kind of assistance?"

"The kind that will help him get done what he wants to get done."

"You mean help getting' rid of Jim Masterson?"

"I mean help," Webster said. "I don't really know what Peacock's intentions are. Only he knows that."

"What are you tellin' me?"

"That I think you did the right thing today," Webster said. "Upon reflection, I mean."

"What?"

"Now that I've thought about it," Webster explained. "There was nothing else you could have done."

Singer looked surprised.

"Thank you, Mayor."

"And when Peacock makes his move," Webster went on, "I think you should do the same thing you did today—stay out of it."

Singer fidgeted in his chair.

"You're tellin' me that Peacock has sent for some gunman to handle Jim Masterson for him—and probably

Neal Brown—and when they get here you want me to do nothin'?"

"I think it would be in your best interest, and the town's," Webster said. "That's all I'm saying."

It took Singer a moment to realize that Webster was done talking, and he had been dismissed.

On the boardwalk in front of City Hall Singer fingered the badge of his chest—the badge that had belonged to Jim Masterson. He had nothing against Masterson. At one time he might even have described them as friends. But he knew once he accepted the job as marshal, he and Jim Masterson were on different sides.

What he had to decide now was just how different the sides truly were.

CHAPTER 53

April 16, 1881

Butler decided to stay in Dodge City for the next week for several reasons. His luck was running so good and he was building up quite a stake for himself. When your luck is going that good you don't want to break it yourself, you have to wait for it to break on its own.

Secondly he wanted to see the results of the telegram he'd sent. He'd figured it would take about a week, so he waited it out.

Ben Thompson, however, had moved on several days before.

"It's quiet," he'd said to Butler, "too quiet, and your damn luck is going too good. Time for me to move on. I know I said I'd watch your back, but that was while I was here."

"You don't need to explain anything to me, Ben," Butler had told him. "You've got to do what's right for you."

"I know you don't want to break your string of luck, Butler, but if I was you I'd leave, too. This quiet ain't gonna last forever. This is what they call a pregnant quiet, if you know what I mean."

"I know what you mean, Ben," Butler had said. "I'll keep it in mind."

"Catch up with you somewhere down the line, then."

The two men shook hands ...

Butler took to sitting in front of the hotel every day now. His mouth started to taste like crap from the cheroots, so he stopped smoking them. Instead, he started whittling. He'd found the same boy who had bought him the first cigars and sent him to buy a block of wood.

"You know what you're doing there?" Neal Brown had asked him the first day he brought out the wood and knife.

"Yep," Butler said. "I'm marking time."

"But can you whittle?" Brown asked. "Do you know what you're doin'?"

"Oh," Butler said, "hell no, I don't."

So for one full morning Neal Brown tried to give Butler a course in whittling. It didn't help much, and the more time that went by, the smaller the piece of wood got, and it resembled nothing. At the end of the afternoon, before he quit his position to go and play cards, Butler would clean up all the wood shavings that had fallen at his feet.

He was, indeed, simply marking time.

Updegraff was getting impatient, but Peacock was not.

"I finally got it figured," Updegraff said to his brother-in-law on the morning of the sixteenth.

"Got what figured?"

"You know when they're getting' here, don't ya? That's why you're not impatient."

Peacock smiled at Updegraff.

"By God, Al, you may not be as dumb as you make out to be."

"So you do know."

Peacock produced a telegram from his desk drawer.

"Got this yesterday. They'll be on the Santa Fe today."

"Jesus Christ!" Updegraff said. "Why didn't you tell me!"

"I told you now," Peacock said. "You and me, we're gonna meet that train, Al. And it's all gonna end today."

"Well, thank God," Updegraff said. "The tension's been killin' me."

Peacock laughed.

"Imagine what it's been doin' to Masterson," he said. "And his friends, Brown and that gambler, too."

"That gambler bothers me," Updegraff said. "He guns that bounty hunter, and then stays in town. For what?"

"The way I hear it, he's cleanin' out every poker player in town."

"Then maybe one of them should get rid of him for us."

"That could still happen," Peacock said, "but stay ready, Al. I'll let you know when we're gonna head for the depot."

"I'll be ready," Updegraff said. "I been ready for this for a long time. I'm gonna put a bullet right in Jim Masterson's back."

* * *

It had not been a good week for Marshal Fred Singer. He was still struggling with what Mayor Webster had told him. He was supposed to stand by and watch Jim Masterson be killed. It didn't sit right with him, but if he did something about it, he'd be switching sides—again. For at one time he'd been perceived as a Masterson supporter, until he'd accepted the badge they'd taken away from Jim. Now, if he switched back, he'd be branding himself as a man who couldn't make up his mind which side he was on.

In truth, he was on Fred Singer's side—he just didn't know, lately, where that put him.

He got up from his desk and walked to the door. Looking out the window he could see the Lady Gay off to his left, and the Dodge House off to his right, where Butler sat each day, whittling. The man looked completely relaxed. Maybe that was what Singer needed to do, sit out in front of his office with a block of wood, and relax. Let whatever was going to happen happen.

He was sure that would not have been Jim Masterson's solution if he was still wearing the marshal's badge.

"Why don't you go and take a walk?" Jim Masterson said to Neal Brown. "You're makin me nervous."

Brown looked across the table at Masterson. They were each nursing a beer. Updegraff was behind the bar, and A. J. Peacock was in the office.

"I got nowhere to go," Brown said. "I think I'll just stay here and keep you alive."

"It's been a quiet week, Neal."

"Too quiet." Brown leaned forward. "Besides, I

happen to know there's a sawed-off behind the bar."

"Updegraff wouldn't have the balls," Masterson said.

"I'm just waitin' for Peacock to leave the office so I can go in."

"What do you do in there, Jim?" Brown asked. "You're not the office type. Even when you were marshal you were never in the office, you were always on the street."

"It's my office, too." Masterson said. "It's not just his."

"Listen to you," Brown said. "You're fightin' over somethin' you don't even want."

"This ain't about a desk, Neal."

Neal Brown spread his arms to indicate the interior of the Lady Gay and said, "I wasn't talkin' about the desk."

Peacock came out of the office, saw that the place had a smattering of patrons, among them Jim Masterson and Neal Brown sitting with their heads together.

He walked over to the bar, waited for Updegraff to finish serving a cowboy, then called him over.

"Go on over to the railroad station and wait for me," he said. "Take your gun."

"You bet I will!"

Peacock put his hand on Updegraff's arm.

"Slowly," he said. "And go out the back."

"Okay." Updegraff started away, then stopped short. "But what about the bar?"

"Lenny's comin' in to man the bar," Peacock said, "Go."

Updegraff nodded, came out from behind the bar and went through a doorway that led to his room near the back. He'd collect his guns and go out the back door.

Peacock got behind the bar to wait for Lenny, one of the other bartenders. Within the hour he'd be going over to the station to await the arrival of Jason Ruger and his men. He considered drawing two beers and taking them over to Masterson and Brown, to celebrate their last day on earth.

Neal Brown saw Peacock get behind the bar and said, "What the hell is that about?"

"I don't know," Masterson said, "but it looks like I can get to the office now." He stood up without looking over at Peacock and turned to head for the office.

"Jim—"

Masterson looked down at his friend and said, "Neal, damn it, take a walk!"

He turned and continued to the office. Neal Brown stared after him, trying not to be angry. His friend was under a lot of pressure. In the end he decided to do what Masterson suggested and get some fresh air.

For the past several days Butler had taken to walking over to the train depot in the afternoon, when the Santa Fe was due in, to wait and see who got off. The train's arrival was still a couple of hours away, but his block of wood—the third one he was working on—was almost gone so he decided just to take the walk.

He put what was left of the wood on the chair and headed for the train station at a slow pace.

CHAPTER 54

As Butler was passing the Lady Gay Neal Brown came out, spotted him, and waved. Butler slowed so the other man could join him.

"Where are you off to?" Brown asked.

"Just walking," Butler lied. "Thought I'd just walk to the train station and back."

"Mind if I join you?"

"Something wrong?"

"Ah," Brown said, falling into step with Butler, "Jim and I are getting' on each other's nerves."

"What about?"

"He thinks I need to give him more room."

"Why don't you?"

"Because he'll get hisself shot."

"It's been a pretty quiet week," Butler said.

"I know," Brown said. "I don't like it. What's been happening with you? Your luck holdin'?"

"Actually, no," Butler said. "I've lost the last two nights. I lose tonight it might be time to move on."

"You'll miss the fireworks."

"You really think there's going to be some?"

"Oh, yeah," Brown said. "It's gonna come to that. Mark my words."

Butler frowned. Even with him in town Masterson and Brown would be outnumbered. He was hoping the man he'd sent the telegram to would arrive, freeing him up to leave with a clear conscience.

"Ain't nobody shot at you in a week," Neal Brown said. "That must be nice."

"Refreshing," Butler said, "would be a better word."

Updegraff left the Lady Gay by the back door and hurried over to the train station. He was wearing his pistol and carrying a rifle. Today was the day he'd been waiting for. He didn't understand why Peacock hadn't done something like this a long time ago.

When he reached the station he mounted the platform, went to the window to talk to the clerk.

"What time's the train due?"

"'bout half an hour," the clerk said, "give or take."

"Give or take what?"

"An hour," the clerk said, and cackled. "Never can tell what's happenin' up the line."

Updegraff scowled and turned away from the man.

When the bartender, Lenny, finally arrived Peacock went straight up to his room to collect his rifle. He also removed the little pocket gun he usually carried, and strapped on his holster. He hadn't used any of his guns in a while, but it wasn't something you forgot how to do, and today ... today was a special occasion.

Jim Masterson couldn't sit at his desk.

For one thing, he didn't think of it as his desk. His desk was over in the marshal's office.

He paced the office, feeling bad about snapping at Neal Brown. The man was his most loyal friend and didn't deserve to be talked to like that. Masterson finally decided to go back out and apologize to him.

When he opened the door and stepped out of the office, he noticed that Brown was gone. He'd probably gone for that walk he'd been pushing him to take.

Masterson decided to go and find his friend and make his apology. As he approached the batwing doors he noticed that Lenny was behind the bar and Peacock was gone.

"Lenny, where's Peacock?"

"Don't know where he is, Mr. Masterson," the bartender said, "but he just left."

"He didn't say where he was goin'?"

"No," Lenny said, "but he was movin' pretty fast as he came down the stairs, and he was carrying his rifle. Sure looked like he was wearing his holster, too."

"Shit," Masterson said beneath his breath, and hurried outside.

"I notice you been sittin' out in front of your hotel all week durin' the day," Brown said. "Just watchin' the town go by?"

"Pretty much."

"I had an idea you might be doin' something' else."

"Like what?"

"Like, maybe, waitin' for somethin'—or somebody."

Butler kept staring straight ahead and didn't comment.

"I also noticed you been takin' this walk over to the station for the past couple of days."

"Have you been watching me, Neal?"

"Ain't had much of anythin' else to do," Brown said, "so I mosey over and look out the window or the door of the Lady Gay, and there you are, walkin' to the station."

Butler didn't comment.

"So, who we waitin' for, Butler?"

They came within sight of the station and Butler noticed something right away.

"What's he doing there?" he asked.

Brown looked ahead and saw what Butler saw.

"Updegraff," Brown said. "Sonofabitch. Him or Peacock—probably Peacock, cause Al ain't got the brains God gave a fly—musta sent for somebody, and they're comin' in on today's train."

"Sent for someone," Butler said. "You mean a gunman?"

"If I know Peacock," Brown said, "and he's desperate enough to do this, it'll be more than one."

"Shit."

"Yeah."

Brown grabbed Butler's arm to stop his progress, turned to face him.

"Time to talk straight, Butler," Brown said. "Who'd you send for?"

"I didn't send for anyone," Butler said. "I sent a telegram, but I don't know if he's coming or not. I've just been ... checking each day to see."

"Is it somebody who's gonna do us some good?"

"I think so."

"Well," Neal Brown said. "We come this far, tell me the rest. Who is it?"

"It's Bat," Butler said. "Bat Masterson."

CHAPTER 55

The air was dead still.

In the distance they could hear the train whistle.

"This could be bad," Brown said. "Peacock's men are probably on that train."

"And we don't know for sure if Bat Masterson is."

"We don't know if Bat's gonna come at all," Brown said. "Jim is gonna be ... I don't know a better word for mad."

"Livid."

"Is that a word?"

"It is."

"It sounds good enough. Does Bat know who sent the telegram?"

"No," Butler said, "I didn't sign it."

"What did it say?"

"'Peacock and Updegraff are planning to kill Jim. Come quick.' Something like that."

"Well," Brown said, "my money is on him comin' after a message like that."

"Yeah, but maybe not on this train."

"Updegraff hasn't seen us yet," Brown said. "We can go around and come at the station from the other side. If Al is here, Peacock will be along. Come on."

By the time they got into position they could see that Peacock had joined Updegraff on the platform. They were both wearing guns and carrying rifles.

"They're not gonna waste any time," Brown said. "As soon as the men they hired get off the train, they'll head for Jim."

"All this just to get rid of Jim Masterson?" Butler said, shaking his head.

"To kill him, not just get rid of him."

The train would pull in any minute.

"If Bat is on that train he's gonna walk right into it," Brown said.

"Yeah, but what are the chances he'll be on this train?" Butler asked. "That'd be some coincidence."

"I'm goin' back around to the other side, now that Peacock's here. If we have to take a hand we might as well do it from both sides."

"Okay."

"If somethin' happens don't wait for me," Brown said. "Do what you gotta do."

"You do the same."

As Brown left to circle back around, Butler took out his gun, checked his loads, and slid it back into his holster just as the train pulled in.

"You know what this fella Ruger looks like?" Updegraff asked.

"Yeah, I know 'im."

"How many is he gonna have with him?"

"Three, I think."

The train pulled in, slowed down, eventually came to a stop. A conductor stepped down to the platform first, and then other passengers. Half a dozen people disembarked—a woman with a child, a couple of men who looked like drummers, a man and his wife—before Peacock saw Jason Ruger step down. He was a tall, wide-shouldered man with a flat-brimmed black hat and a black vest. Three men stepped off right after him, and looked to him for their next step. Ruger looked down the platform and saw Peacock, who waved.

"Okay," Peacock said, "this is it. Let's go meet 'em. They'll need to get their horses from the stock car."

As they started down the platform Peacock saw a man step down several cars beyond Ruger and his men. He recognized the man, and couldn't believe his eyes.

"Damn!" he said.

"What?" Updegraff asked.

"It's Goddamned Bat Masterson!"

"Where?" Updegraff asked, looking around wildly. For a man who claimed not to be afraid of Bat Masterson, he was already sweating.

Butler saw the man from the back, but instinctively knew it was Bat Masterson. He saw that Peacock had recognized him as well. Both he and Updegraff pulled their guns and Peacock shouted to other men on the platform, "Bat Masterson!"

Ruger heard the word Masterson. He didn't cared if it was Jim or Bat, all he cared about was getting paid. He saw Peacock and the man with him draw their guns, and turned to his men.

"This is it!" he said.

Well trained, none of his men complained, nor did he, about how fast they were being pressed into service.

They all drew their guns, and suddenly six men were facing a surprised Bat Masterson.

Neal Brown saw what was happening, and was too far to help Bat right away. He had to get closer. He drew his gun and mounted the platform.

"Watch out, Masterson!" Butler shouted, running up onto the platform, gun in hand.

He didn't wait for Bat to react. He fired off a shot immediately, and one of Ruger's men caught the bullet on the hip and spun around.

Bat heard the warning shout behind him, but his hand was already streaking to his gun. Somehow Peacock knew he was on the train, and had a welcome set up for him. He had no time to think, just to react.

He drew and fired.

Jim Masterson heard the train pull in at the end of town. It didn't occur to him that Neal Brown might be there until he heard the shots.

"Damn it!" he snarled, and started running.

Fred Singer heard the train and shots, also, from his office. He sat behind his desk. Hands clenched into fists and eyes closed.

* * *

Ruger and his men dove for cover, as did Peacock and Updegraff. But Neal Brown came up behind the two brothers-in-law and shouted, "Peacock!"

Updegraff and Peacock turned, saw Brown and raised their guns. Brown fired, and caught Updegraff in the chest. The man immediately went down on his back.

Peacock dropped to one knee and raised his gun to fire.

Butler reached Bat and stood shoulder to shoulder with him.

"Who're you?" Bat demanded.

"A friend."

"Ain't gonna argue with that now," Bat Masterson said.

They both fired until their guns were empty, then sought cover while they reloaded. Bat got back on the train, and Butler ducked behind a bench, moving it so it afforded him some cover.

"Who's that at the other end of the platform?" Bat called out.

"Neal Brown!"

"Where's my brother? Is he alive?"

"He was at the Lady Gay."

"If I know Jim," Bat yelled, "he'll be here any minute and be mad if we don't save him some action."

Butler snapped the cylinder closed on his reloaded weapon and said, "Hell, he can have as much of it as he wants, for all I care!"

CHAPTER 56

Bat was wearing two guns, and reloaded both from the cover of the railroad car. From the other end of the platform there was still gunfire.

"I'm gonna jump down from the other side of the train and circle around," Bat told Butler.

"Go," Butler said. "I'll keep them busy from here."

Bat palmed both guns, moved through to the other side of the train, and dropped down to the ground.

Butler saw Ruger's men moving toward him, moving from car to car, cover to cover, and knew he'd have to move as well. He fired off two shots, then turned and made his way to the end of the platform again. He was going to circle the depot again, then decided to go around the train and join Bat. He fired off the rest of his shots, then made for the train, once again reloading.

When Jim Masterson reached the train station, lead was flying all over. He saw Neal Brown backing up on the platform, moving toward him, returning fire, and went to join him.

"What the hell is goin' on?" he shouted.

"Peacock," Brown said. "He's tryin' to kill Bat, him and some gunnies he hired."

"Bat's here?"

Brown nodded. "Got off the train."

Peacock was firing from cover, and behind him Ruger joined him. Jim Masterson saw the hat and vest, and the cut of the man's figure, and said, "He hired Jason Ruger."

"Ruger? Is that who it is?"

"How many men with him?"

"He got off the train with three, then there's Peacock and Updegraff."

"Updegraff! Where?"

"I put him down."

"Who's at the other end of the platform?"

"Bat and Butler."

"Butler, too? That makes it four to six. Not bad."

Brown and Jim backed down the steps of the platform to use them for cover. The train station was at the end of Front Street, so behind them some of the buildings were taking lead. Suddenly, Bat appeared from behind the engine, and behind him Butler. The joined Jim and Brown.

"Bat," Jim said.

"Jim. Got yourself into some trouble, I see."

"I thought you were the one in trouble."

"It don't matter!" Brown said.

"He's right," Bat agreed. He turned and looked at Butler. "Who are you?"

"His name's Butler," Jim said. "He's a friend."

"So he told me."

The four men conversed while returning fire from up the platform.

"Let's take this off the platform," Jim suggested, "and into town."

"Gonna be some damage," Bat said.

"Fuck 'em," Jim said, "they fired us."

"Let's go, then. Will they follow?"

"Oh, yeah," Jim said. "Peacock wants to finish this."

"Your partner?" Bat asked, confused.

"Not anymore."

The four men backed away, then turned and headed down Front Street. Making a stand would be easier out in the open.

"They're runnin'," Ruger said to Peacock. "Do we let them go?"

"No!" Peacock said. "I brought you here to do some killin'. They're just takin' the fight into town."

"What about the local law?"

"Not a problem," Peacock said. "Just earn your money."

"Let's go after 'em, then."

He turned and waved for his men to follow. They obeyed, even the one with a bullet in his hip. Peacock let them all go first, and then moved in behind them. He didn't know if Updegraff was dead on the platform, but he wasn't worried about it at the moment.

The gun battle spilled onto the street. Jim's plan at first had been to hit-and-run, move from cover to cover, but suddenly he was cool, not angry.

"Let's just stand and take 'em," he said.

"Suits me," Neal Brown said. "I been wantin' to put a bullet into your partner for months."

"Butler?" Jim said.

"I'm with you."

"Bat?"

"Why the hell not?" Bat said. "I don't know what the hell is goin' on, anyway."

By the time Ruger, his men, and Peacock made their way to Front Street, Bat, Jim, Neal Brown, and Butler were fanned out in the street.

Peacock, Ruger, and his men stopped in their tracks.

"Come and get it," Jim Masterson said.

The streets were empty. The townspeople had taken cover at the first sound of shots. There was nobody with a badge to be seen anywhere. Dodge City had suddenly become a ghost town, but if you looked closely you'd see faces in almost every window. Scared off the streets, folks were not too frightened to want to watch the action.

"That sonofabitch Singer," Neal Brown said.

"Fred Singer?" Bat asked.

"He's the new marshal," Jim said. "He's stayin' away from this, probably on orders from the new mayor."

"New mayor, new marshal," Bat said. "A whole lot of things *have* changed."

"And a whole lot have stayed the same," Jim said.

The two brothers were standing shoulder to shoulder, Neal Brown to Jim's right, Butler to Bat's left.

"Think they'll turn a run?" Bat asked.

"They're probably getting' paid a lot of money for

this," Jim said. "Enough so that your legend won't intimidate them."

"Well, hell," Bat said, "what good is it, then?"

"Here they come," Butler said.

Lead and gunsmoke filled the air, but only one was lethal.

The two groups of men advanced on each other, firing as they came. All were cool in the face of danger, but the Mastersons, Neal Brown, and Butler were more deadly accurate with their weapons.

Ruger's men, supposedly experienced, fired quickly and wildly. As hot bits of lead flew around one tore through Butler coat, singing his side. The gambler fired coolly, putting one of Ruger's men down. Bullets could be heard striking the sides of buildings and breaking glass. Some of the townspeople watching from their windows were forced to scatter. Later Butler would wonder about those wild shots, would come to the conclusion that faced with imminent death at the hands of men like the Masterson brothers and Neal Brown, even the most professional of men could panic.

Ruger's men fell one by one, Butler, the Mastersons and Neal Brown continuing to waste little or no lead. Finally, Ruger himself was struck by several shots—they'd argue later over whose—and joined his men on the ground.

The gunfire stopped.

The smoke floated up and away, turning into tendrils as it drifted higher and higher.

"Where the hell is Peacock?" Neal Brown demanded.

Jim Masterson's partner was nowhere to be found.

CHAPTER 57

On the day he was to leave town Butler stopped in at Hank's café for breakfast.

Several days had passed since the shooting. Ruger and his men had been killed, Updegraff wounded, both he and Peacock ... gone. No one knew where, or heard from them again. The mayor had tried to have Bat and Jim Masterson arrested, but since Singer had not witnessed any wrongdoing, he did not make any arrests.

Hank prepared a steak-and-egg breakfast for Butler and sat with him while he ate it.

"So you checked out of your hotel?" Hank asked.

Butler nodded.

"Time for me to move on."

"I'll bet the Mastersons were grateful for your help."

"They probably would have done just as well without me."

"Did they ever find out who sent that telegram to Bat Masterson in Tombstone?"

"No," Butler said. Neal Brown had agreed to keep his

mouth shut. It would go down in history as an anonymous telegram.

"So where are you headed?"

"West. The next place. I'll probably make Tombstone, Denver, some other places along the way, and end up in San Francisco. What about you?"

"What about me?"

"You going to stay here?"

"Probably."

"Wait for someone else to recognize you?"

"Might not happen."

"I hope it doesn't."

Next to Butler's plate was the copy of the *Dodge City Times* containing the story of the shooting. "The Battle of the Plaza," M. J. Healy had called it. Butler didn't know where the plaza was, but it was as good a name as any for her big story. He'd told her everything he knew in return for one thing—she left his name out. As far as anyone who read the story knew, it was Bat and Jim Masterson along with Neal Brown.

"What are the Mastersons gonna do?" Hank asked.

"Bat's already gone," Butler said. "Jim's going to sell, and he and Neal Brown will leave."

"This town might actually end up bein' borin'," Hank said.

"That would be a switch."

After breakfast Hank walked Butler to the door.

"So everybody's satisfied," the cook said. "The mayor will be happy once Jim Masterson leaves."

"Dog Kelley will run his saloon, maybe run for office again next time."

"I'd vote for him," Hank said, "if I was a voter."

"So you'll be happy here?" Butler asked.

"For now."

The two men shook hands and Butler started to leave.

"Wait!"

"What is it?"

"You kept that bounty hunter away from me, Butler," Hank said. "I owe you for that."

"You don't owe me anything, Hank—"

"It's Henry," the man said, "Henry Plummer."

"Henry ... Plummer?"

Plummer waited to see if it would sink in.

"Didn't I read something about ... Montana?"

"Bannock," Plummer said, "and Virginia City."

"And you were supposed to have been hanged in ... sixty ... three?"

"Four," Plummer said. "A lot of years ago."

"Where have you been all this time?"

"Movin'," Plummer said. "Job to job, name to name, until I got here."

"Well," Butler said, "everybody deserves a second chance, Henry. Your secret is safe with me."

"I know it," Plummer said. "Take care your own secrets don't catch up with you."

"They always do," Butler said, "but I've learned to survive."

"I've been doin' that for years," Henry Plummer said. "Take my advice, Butler ... learn how to live."

AUTHOR'S NOTE

The gun battle at the end of this book was known as "Too Much Blood" and "The Battle of the Plaza." It did not happen exactly as I have depicted here. I changed it to fit Butler into the mix. The other principals—except Ruger and his men, who are my creations—actually were in Dodge City at the time.

Ben Thompson spent a lot of time in Dodge, maybe just not when I had him there.

Henry Plummer, as far as anyone knows, was hung in 1864 for his crimes against the towns of Bannock and Virginia City, Montana—committed while he was sheriff. There is a rumor he escaped hanging and went into hiding, but no one knows for sure.

The telegram sent to Bat Masterson in Tombstone was real, and has always been attributed to an anonymous source. That just made it easy for me to give the credit to my character, Butler. The telegram was part of the reason Bat Masterson was not in Tombstone during the O.K. Corral.

But he had his own Battle of the Plaza.